# On Edge

Sarah Lawson

Published by Lechner Syndications

www.lechnersyndications.com

Copyright © 2014 Sarah Lawson

ISBN 13: 978-1-927794-21-0

"I was passionate. I found something that I loved. I could be all alone in a big old skating rink and nobody could get near me and I didn't have to talk to anybody because of my shyness. It was great. I was in my fantasy world."

~Dorothy Hamill

.

# CONTENTS

Chapter  1        Pg # 1

Chapter  2        Pg # 7

Chapter  3        Pg # 13

Chapter  4        Pg # 19

Chapter  5        Pg # 25

Chapter  6        Pg # 31

Chapter  7        Pg # 41

Chapter  8        Pg # 53

Chapter  9        Pg # 59

Chapter 10        Pg # 69

Chapter 11        Pg # 77

Chapter 12        Pg # 89

Chapter 13        Pg # 99

Chapter 14        Pg # 111

Chapter 15        Pg # 123

Chapter 16        Pg # 133

Chapter 17        Pg # 141

# CHAPTER 1

*Pro: She has the ice (almost) to herself on this last week of summer vacation.*
*Con: It's no fun to skate without her bestie, Hannah.*

Madison Boone took another lap around the deserted rink at the Emerald City Skate Club, her blades carving into the ice as she gained momentum. Turning backward, Maddie skated three more hard strokes and planted her toe pick into the ice, feeling the burn in her quadriceps as she propelled her body upward into a triple Lutz jump. She knew she was in trouble after only two revolutions. While her brain willed her body to keep twisting in the air, somehow her skates didn't get the memo. She crashed hard, gasping as her hip hit the ice. The cold penetrated her black leggings and she scrambled to get up, determined to try again. That was the third time she'd missed the landing today.

"Wait," called out her coach. Max Baer skated toward her, wearing his trademark blue fleece vest over a t-shirt and Adidas sweat pants. He glided to a stop, concern evident in the creases between his eyebrows. "You're a million miles away today, Maddie."

A strand of honey-blond hair had slipped free from her ponytail and she tucked it behind her ear. "What do you mean?"

"I know you can land that jump," he said, traces of his German accent clinging to his words. "I've seen you do it many times. Why are you distracted?"

"I'll keep trying." Maddie planted her hands on her hips and looked past him. On the other side of the rink, Maddie's teammate and friend, Alyssa McDonnell, skated alongside a beginning skater. The little girl was adorable. From her pale pink leotard and gauzy skirt, to her beige tights and sparkling white skates, she listened to Alyssa with rapt attention. Then she attempted a basic bunny hop, her face lighting up when Alyssa praised her efforts. A twinge of envy caught Maddie by surprise. Sometimes she longed for the days when jumps were that simple.

"You haven't answered my question." Max leaned into her field of vision. "What's on your mind?"

Maddie shrugged. "That camp was full of incredibly talented skaters. I guess I'm kind of intimidated."

Max nodded. "I understand. But that's what camp is for, remember? You spent two weeks with the best and most promising skaters in the whole western United States. Very few girls your age get to do that."

"You sound like my parents," Maddie said. She'd had more than one late night cry fest with her mother in their hotel room, bawling about how the other skaters were amazing. Everyone at the rink stopped to watch Sydney Gray from Colorado land her triple-triple flawlessly. Over and over. Skate camp was definitely a wake-up call. Maddie had a lot of work to do if she wanted to make it to the National Championships in Omaha. And she did.

"If your mother was here, she'd give you a list—all the pros and cons to nailing a triple Lutz." A half-smile played at the corner of Max's lips and he clapped his hand on her shoulder.

Maddie couldn't help but smile. "Her problem-solving skills are epic."

"That they are." Max skated backward in a half circle. "Show me a triple flip and a double Axel, and then grab some water."

*Yes.* Maddie pumped her fist in the air. She and Hannah Springer, her best friend and fellow skater at Emerald City Skate Club, had practiced the triple flip last week until their legs were like Jell-O. Pushing off, she skated away from Max, looping around the rink as her t-shirt rippled in the cool air. Twisting backward, she skated a series of crossovers effortlessly, the familiar cadence of her blades carving into the ice sending a rush of adrenaline through her. Gliding on one leg, she jammed her other toe pick into the ice and jumped into the air. Visions of Sydney Gray soaring across the ice at camp flashed in her head, right before her own blades tangled and she landed in a heap on the ice. *What in the world?*

She didn't have to look at Max to know he was disappointed. His muttering in German said it all. This was not her day. And where was Hannah when she really needed her? The struggles and frustrations of a grueling practice were always easier to handle when she and her BFF, Hannah Springer, could hang out and vent afterward.

Maddie got up and skated toward the edge of the rink, where Max's wife, Elise, waited on the other side of the boards.

"It's going to be okay." Elise passed her a water bottle and offered a sympathetic smile.

Maddie twisted the cap off the bottle and took a long pull, watching as Max skated toward Alyssa and her young student. That was never a good sign, when he skated off without saying a word she could understand.

"Don't worry about him," Elise said. "He knows you are capable of landing these jumps and he just wants you to do your best."

"I'm really trying, Elise. I don't know what's wrong." Maddie set the bottle down and reached for her inhaler. She hadn't struggled with an asthma attack in recent weeks, but she wasn't taking any chances.

"You're probably exhausted. Camp takes a lot out of you."

Maddie followed her medication with another sip of water, hoping Elise was right. If she got some rest, settled back into her normal routine—everything would fall into place, right? How she wished Hannah was here. "Do you know where Hannah is today?"

Elise's smile faded and an emotion Maddie couldn't quite discern flickered in her coach's eyes. An awkward silence hung between them. "Something came up. I—I'm not exactly sure what's going on with Hannah."

The fine hairs on Maddie's arms stood on end. That was weird. She'd ridden home from the airport with Hannah yesterday and she hadn't mentioned anything. Hannah never missed an opportunity to skate. Her mother made sure of that. "Do you think she's okay?"

"I'm sure she's fine. C'mon, let's end today on a positive note. Why don't you take a lap and then give me your best spin?"

"Any spin?"

Elise nodded. "Any spin."

"Got it." Maddie skated away, eager to prove to her coaches and herself that she could execute at least one element well today. The new, complex scoring system for figure skating emphasized the grade of execution on almost every component now. That meant she couldn't afford to make many mistakes in competition, especially during sectionals and regionals. *One day at a time.* Taking a deep breath, she worked in some of her more intricate footwork from her short program, and then glided across the ice in a spread eagle. She finished with a camel spin, the worries and concerns of her workout churning away as she spun like a top. Jamming her toe pick into the ice once again, she came to a stop and thrust her arms in the air. *There.* That's more like it.

Elise clapped and whistled. "There you go! Nicely done."

Chest heaving, Maddie skated off the ice, both proud of herself and relieved to be finished for the day. She chugged the rest of her water before sinking onto the bench on the other side of the boards. Max had left the ice and she could see him pacing near the locker room, his cell phone pressed to his ear.

"Have you and your mom agreed on an outfit for your short program?" Elise leaned against the boards, twisting her long dark hair into a messy bun. "I know she has some opinions about that."

Maddie tucked her empty water bottle inside her bag. "She wants me to wear red. I think teal green would be better."

"Green would be pretty. Brings out the color in those beautiful hazel eyes of yours."

"Mom says red demands attention, captivates the audience."

"Blondes look fabulous in red, that's for sure. I know you'll work it out." Elise waved a hand in the air, as if to dismiss any concern. As if it were that easy.

"So what was your favorite part about camp?" Elise asked.

Maddie loosened her tights and tugged at the laces on her skates. "I had a chance to meet Michele Kwan during a break-out session. That was pretty sweet."

"Good for you. Did you take a picture?"

Maddie smiled. "Maybe a couple. She said I could post them on Instagram, too."

"That's awesome. The first time I met one of my skating heroes, I burst into tears." Elise shook her head. "I can't believe I did that."

"She seemed so normal. I didn't really think of her as, like, a decorated Olympian until I was telling my mom about it later on."

"I'm glad you played it cool, then. Good job today, we'll see you tomorrow." Elise squeezed her shoulder and moved toward the rink manager's office at the end of the arena. Max was nowhere in sight.

Maddie cleaned her skate blades with a cloth she kept in her duffle bag. Tucking them inside, she pulled on her tennis shoes and checked her smartphone for messages. A text from Hannah illuminated the screen.

I've got big news. Can your family meet mine at Randy's for pizza later?

Maddie moved toward the mats to stretch her weary muscles, her fingers flying over the screen in response. Where are you? Why did you skip practice?

Dropping her bag to the floor, she sat down on the mat and reached for her toes. While she waited for Hannah's answer, she fired off a quick text to her mom to make plans for pizza. Sitting upright, she stared at her phone, willing an update to appear. A new message appeared:

Huge news. I can't wait to tell you everything.

Maddie sighed and dropped her phone onto the mat. She reached for her toes once again, trying to ignore the anxious knot forming in her stomach. Somehow she had a feeling Hannah's news would be anything but good.

# CHAPTER 2

*Pro: Surprises are fun, especially if they involve your family and very best friend.*
*Con: Surprises stink when it means your whole world is crashing down.*

Maddie waved goodbye to Max and Elise, slung her duffle bag over her shoulder and pushed through the front door of the Emerald City Skate Club. Mom's silver Toyota Sequoia waited at the curb. Maddie jogged to the passenger side and pulled open the door.

"Where's Hannah?"

Mom looked up from her smartphone, green eyes flashing. "Hi, Mom. How was your day?"

Maddie rolled her eyes and climbed into the passenger seat. "Hi. Hannah says she has huge news. What's going on?"

Caroline Boone sighed and slid her phone back inside her Coach handbag. Tucking her smooth, platinum blonde bob behind one ear, she shifted the car into drive. "I don't know. Mrs. Springer never said a word. Whatever it is, it must be a big surprise."

Maddie's stomach churned as she reached for her seat belt and clicked it in place. A surprise? They'd just flown home from camp, after spending almost every minute together for two solid weeks. Hannah told her everything … didn't she? Pulling her smartphone out of her bag, she swiped her finger across the screen. No new texts from Hannah. Maddie sent another one to her.

"Their timing couldn't be worse," Mom said, checking both ways before pulling out into traffic. "We've got laundry to do, your dad has a four o'clock patient, and Emily needs your help with some new clients. Ray's is the last place we need to be tonight."

"New clients?" Maddie stared at her phone, willing a text message to materialize.

"She heard the Clarks have a new pet. I sent her over to get the details."

Maddie groaned. Their pet sitting service was fun—most of the time—but this was a busy season with everyone squeezing in their last vacation before school started. Emily's love for animals knew no bounds, but Maddie shared half the workload and there weren't enough hours in the day for more walks or play sessions. She chewed on her lower lip. There'd be plenty of time to worry about that later. Right now she needed to figure out what was up with Hannah.

"Let's look at the bright side: they've always got great ideas for ways to improve things for the club. Maybe they want to talk about fundraising for regionals and sectionals."

"That's, like, two months from now, Mom."

"The Springers like to plan ahead, you know that. Maybe Dr. Springer is making a big donation."

"I've got a bad feeling about this. I don't think it's the good kind of surprise."

"Frankly, there's no such thing as a good surprise as far as I'm concerned." Mom clicked on her turn signal and pulled into the center lane to merge onto the freeway. "I can't stand surprises."

Traffic crawled as they made their way down I-5. Maddie checked Facebook and Instagram, but Hannah hadn't posted anything since they left California. Maybe Mom was right. As the parents of an only child, it would be like Dr. and Mrs. Springer to dissect the abilities of every skater in the western US over pizza on a Friday night and formulate a plan to compete against them. Hannah often ducked her head, two apples of color tinging her high cheekbones, while they over-analyzed numerous short programs pulled up on YouTube.

Mom tapped a manicured fingernail on the gear shift while they waited. "I wonder if Dr. Springer is opening his own practice? They've talked about that forever."

"I hope so," Maddie whispered, staring out the window. Sunlight reflected off Lake Washington, sailboats and jet skis already out on the water for what promised to be a gorgeous late summer weekend.

As they exited the freeway and climbed the hill toward Preston Heights, Maddie scrolled through the pictures on her phone. Skating competitions, silly moments at practice, rare shopping trips to the mall—Hannah was in almost every one. Since the first day they met on the ice several years before, they'd been practically inseparable. Her stomach twisted in an anxious knot. She knew everything there was to know about Hannah. Right?

At the entrance to their neighborhood, Magnolia Ridge, Mom slowed down as a moving truck passed through the wrought iron gates. A man in khaki pants and a red polo shirt stood at the end of the first driveway, beckoning for the driver to come closer.

"Are those the new neighbors?"

Mom slowed the car and waited for the truck to pull out of the street. "I think so. Maybe I'll stop by while you're getting ready and say hello."

"Okay. I'll try to hurry." Maddie couldn't remember the last time a new family moved into the neighborhood. With its views of the lake and spacious lots, Magnolia Ridge was home to many doctors, lawyers, and Microsoft executives. Maddie noticed Emily's scooter lying on the lawn in front of their own two-story brick home. Maybe the Clarks had changed their mind and they'd have one less chore to do this weekend.

Mom opened the garage door with the remote clipped to her visor and eased the car inside. Maddie hopped out of the car as soon as it stopped and raced into the house. The suspense was killing her. The faster she got ready, the sooner they could be on their way to Ray's and get the scoop.

Emily glanced up from the leather sofa in the living room. She was watching Animal Planet on television and eating a slice of watermelon.

"I thought you went to see the Clarks' new pet?" Maddie asked, hanging her duffle bag on the hook in the mud room.

"It's a parakeet. Not interested," Emily said, eyes glued to the screen.

"Sweet." Maddie kicked off her shoes, not even trying to conceal her disappointment. "Are you coming with us to Ray's? We're having pizza with Hannah."

Emily wrinkled her nose. "No, thanks. Zak is taking me to the movies."

"Zak? Really?" Their older brothers rarely made time to go anywhere with them, especially in the summer. Nicholas was so busy spending time with his friends before he left for Stanford that they hardly ever saw him.

"Yep. He owes me. I did his chores last week while he was at camp if he'd take me to the movies tonight."

Maddie laughed. For an eleven-year-old, Emily was quite the businesswoman. "Mom will be back in a few minutes. She went to meet the new neighbors."

"Cool. I hope they have a puppy."

Maddie cringed and headed for her room, taking the stairs two at a time. *Hope they don't.* Pushing open the door to her bedroom, she popped her phone into the docking station on her nightstand. Scrolling through her apps, she pulled up Pandora. The latest Katy Perry hit blasted from the speakers.

After a quick shower, Maddie pulled on favorite purple V-neck t-shirt and cut-off jean shorts. Twisting her damp hair into a bun, she slipped on her white Converse sneakers—minus the laces—and hurried back downstairs. Then she realized she'd forgotten her phone and went back to get it.

Mom was downstairs, giving Emily an update on the new neighbors.

"Guess what, Mads?" Emily beamed, jumping up from the sofa. "The new neighbors are getting a puppy. Mom gave them our number, too."

"Seriously?" Maddie paused on the bottom step, glancing at Mom for clarification.

"The Gray family, moving here from Colorado. Twins—a boy and a girl—who will be sophomores at Preston Heights. Their dog passed a few months ago and he promised them a puppy when they moved in."

"Are the twins here?" Maddie thought about Sydney Gray, a girl at skate camp who dazzled them all with her explosive jumps and amazing talent. She was from Colorado, wasn't she?

"Not yet. They are driving up from Colorado with their mom. I gave them our number, thought Zak could stop by and introduce himself before school starts."

"What about me?" Emily asked. "I want to meet the new puppy."

"Relax," Mom said. "I'm sure they'll call if they need your pet sitting services."

"Come on, Mom." Maddie tilted her head toward the garage. "The Springers are probably waiting."

"Did Hannah text you?" Mom pulled her own phone from her Kate Spade handbag and glanced at the screen.

"No." Maddie sighed. "That's why I want to get over there."

"Let's go, then." Mom planted a kiss on Emily's hair. "Have fun at the movies, sweetie."

On their way out of the neighborhood, Maddie watched two of the movers carrying boxes into the new neighbor's house. She studied the man in the khaki pants and red polo shirt, standing in the garage and gesturing with his hands. Could that really be Sydney Gray's dad? Add that to her list of things to worry about. If she had to live in the same zip code as one of the best figure skaters she'd ever seen, it was going to be a rough year.

"I hope you and Zak can stop by when the kids get here," Mom said.

"Zak can." Maddie gnawed on her thumbnail.

"What are you worried about? Besides Hannah."

"Because Sydney Gray was one of the best skaters we saw at camp. She was from Colorado. What if that's her family? I don't want her living in my neighborhood or—"

Mom reached across the console and patted Maddie's shoulder. "I doubt that's the same family. Gray is a pretty common name."

"How do you know? Did you ask if his daughter skated?"

"Well, no, but—"

"See? You don't actually know it isn't her, then, do you?" Maddie linked her arms across her chest and stared out the window. She hated the way her voice went up an octave and sounded all whiny. Mom obviously wasn't crazy about spending her Friday evening at Ray's, either. But seeing her toughest competition every day at school was almost more than she could handle right now.

"Try to see it from her perspective. Would you want to move to another state in the middle of high school?"

Maddie sighed, relieved that Mom didn't give her a lecture about her attitude. "No, I guess not."

"Whether that's Sydney Gray and her brother or not, we need to be polite and welcome them to our neighborhood. Even if you don't see each other often, you need to use your good manners."

"Okay, okay." The neon sign for Ray's pizza and burgers came into view. Mom turned into the parking lot. Maddie's chest tightened. Hannah stood under the blue-and-white-striped awning outside the front door. Maddie waved and Hannah raised her hand, but her smile waivered.

"I've got a bad feeling about this, Mom." Maddie clutched her phone and hopped out of the car.

Hannah jogged toward her, straight black hair bouncing across her shoulders. "Maddie, you'll never guess what happened."

Maddie swallowed hard and took a few tentative steps toward her best friend. "Why didn't you answer my texts?"

"Mom said I had to tell you in person. Brenda MacPherson called today. She wants to coach me. We're moving to California. Can you believe it?"

Everything moved in slow motion. Hannah's chocolate-brown eyes were wide and she blew her blunt-cut bangs out of her eyes while she waited expectantly for Maddie's response.

# CHAPTER 3

*Pro: Being a great friend means celebrating your friend's success ... right?*
*Con: Hard to be happy when it breaks your heart.*

"Moving? Wait. What?" Hot tears pricked Maddie's eyelids. How can this be?

"Isn't it crazy? I still can't believe it." Hannah's tiny frame practically hummed with excitement. *Why was she so happy? Anyone could see this was a disaster.*

"Hi, Hannah. What's new?" Mom stood beside Maddie, clicking the button on her key fob to automatically lock the car.

"Hey, Mrs. Boone. We're moving to California so I can train with Brenda MacPherson. Isn't that amazing?" Hannah clapped her hands while she bounced up and down.

Maddie bit her lip and glanced at her mom. There weren't words.

Mom cleared her throat and forced a smile. "Wow, Hannah. Congratulations. That's, um, big news."

"Thanks. I know, right?" She grabbed Maddie's hand. "C'mon, let's go in. Mom's got a table for us by the window. You're dad's already here."

The window view from Ray's. Right. How many times had their families shared a meal there together? Maddie wanted to turn and run straight back to the car. Drive home and forget this conversation even happened.

"Let's go inside, honey." Mom slipped her arms around Maddie's shoulders. "We'll get through this, don't worry."

Maddie's Converse shoes felt as if they were filled with concrete as she trailed Hannah into the restaurant. Her palms were cool and clammy. This couldn't be happening. They weaved between the tables until they found Mrs. Springer sitting at a rectangular table, the lake stretching out behind her in the distance. Her dad stood up and came around the table to give her a hug.

"Hi, sweetheart." He pulled her in close, his turquoise-blue scrubs cool against her cheek.

"Hi, dad," Maddie looked up into his blue eyes, reflecting back love and concern for her. Maybe Dad could talk some sense into Mrs. Springer.

"Hi, Maddie. Caroline," Mrs. Springer stood and hugged them both, her flowery perfume wafting toward Maddie's nose. She stiffened, refusing to hug her back. Dad moved past her and gave Mom a kiss on the cheek.

"Maddie, say something," Hannah pleaded. "Anything. Aren't you a little bit excited?"

Maddie stood, frozen, heat crawling up her neck as both Mrs. Springer and Hannah stared at her. "I-I don't know. I guess. A little."

"This is quite a shock," Mom said, pulling out a chair and sinking into it. "We had no idea you were even considering a move."

Maddie eased into a chair next to Mom, putting some distance between herself and her friend. Hurt and frustration battled against a sense of loyalty to Hannah. They'd shared everything together and this was a huge opportunity. Still—

"We didn't think it was even a remote possibility," Mrs. Springer tossed her long blond hair over her shoulder. "Then Brenda saw Hannah skate at camp last week and spoke to us after one of the break-out sessions. One thing led to another and here we are." Mrs. Springer threw her hands up in the air, the huge diamond on her left ring finger catching the light that streamed through the window.

"Do you have to commit right away? I get that it's flattering for her to call you, but do you have to say yes?" Dr. Boone asked, sitting back down in his seat across from Maddie.

"Of course we're saying yes, Emmitt." Mrs. Springer narrowed her gaze. "We'd be foolish to pass this up."

"But what about school?" Maddie cut a glance at Hannah. They were supposed to navigate the treacherous waters of freshman year together.

"Well—" Hannah's eyes flitted toward her mom.

"I'm going to homeschool her," Mrs. Springer chimed in. "We feel that's the best option, given the demands of training for the Olympics full time."

"Samantha, you can't be serious," Mom said.

An awkward silence blanketed the table.

Mrs. Springer pressed her lips into a thin line and twisted her water glass in a circle. "I most certainly am, Caroline. You know the Olympics have always been our goal for Hannah."

Maddie squirmed in her seat. This was so awkward. Of course they dreamed of skating at the Olympics someday—even imagined standing on the podium with their giant bouquets of roses and singing the national anthem. But moving? Uprooting to train with the most sought-after coach in the sport? Maddie knew her parents would never go for that.

"I applaud your efforts to seize the day and do what's best for Hannah, but this is going to take some getting used to." Mom patted Maddie's arm. "For all of us."

"What's Brent going to do?" Dad planted both elbows on the table, rearranging the condiments in the center of the table.

"He'll stay here and work, of course. His skills as a hand surgeon are very much in demand, as I'm sure you know."

Maddie's gasp was audible.

"Lots of skaters do it, Mads." Hannah insisted.

"When will you see him?" Maddie glanced from Hannah to her own dad and back to Hannah. She could never imagine leaving her family behind, not even for skating.

"Holidays, occasional weekends … we'll figure it out," Mrs. Springer said. "Speaking of, where is he?" She pulled her smartphone from her Kate Spade purse and stared at the screen. "He must be stuck in surgery."

"What does he think of all this?" Mom asked.

"He's very supportive, naturally. He wants what's best for Hannah." Mrs. Springer tucked her phone back in her bag.

"Have you told Max and Elise?" Maddie remembered their strange response to her questions about Hannah at practice. Now this all made more sense.

"We're meeting with them first thing tomorrow."

Maddie cringed. They'd be crushed. Hannah's huge smile and amazing talent made skating look so fun and effortless. Emerald City Skate Club wouldn't be the same without her.

The waiter arrived at the table and took their drink orders.

"Do you need a few more minutes to decide?" He gazed around the table.

Maddie wasn't in the mood for pizza, even though she rarely splurged on heavy carbs. Her stomach still churned as she processed Hannah's news.

"What do you think, Mads?" Dad asked. "A large veggie?"

Maddie shrugged. "Whatever. I'm not very hungry."

"So, Maddie, you'll have to come visit us." Mrs. Springer offered a smile as she reached for her water glass.

"We just got back from California," Mom said. "With school starting soon, I can't imagine when she'll have time for a trip like that."

There was an edge to her voice and Maddie cheered silently. *Go, Mom.* Despite the pep talk in the car about good manners, Maddie was pleased her Mom was making her feelings known. This sucked. Big time.

"This isn't goodbye forever," Hannah said. "We'll see each other sometimes. Besides, there's always FaceTime and Skype, right?"

Maddie jumped up, her chair clattering to the floor. "I can't do this." Tears blurred her vision as she bolted toward the front door, ignoring Mom's pleas for her to come back.

Outside the restaurant, people milled around, waiting for a table to open up. Maddie pushed past them, jogging down the cement path to the terrace behind the restaurant. She didn't know where else to go but she definitely wasn't going back in there. She kept jogging, swiping at the tears that trickled down her cheeks. The path eventually ran out and she sank onto a wooden bench overlooking the water.

A light breeze was blowing and she shivered. Even if the skies opened up and poured buckets—which seemed unlikely, given there wasn't a cloud in sight—she still wasn't going back inside. The feelings she'd held in check rose to the surface, like a fissure in a dam cracking wide open, and she tucked her knees up under her chin and let the tears fall. So not fair. Hannah Springer was the most selfish, inconsiderate person she'd ever met. If they never spoke to each other again, it would be too soon.

# CHAPTER 4

*Pro: Is there anything more adorable than a puppy to cheer a girl up?*
*Con: What if the puppy's owner is such a hottie that you totally say something dumb?*

The porch swing creaked as Maddie pushed off with her foot, swaying back and forth. The fountain in her parents' new water feature trickled and babbled a soothing background noise for her one-woman pity party. She clutched a pillow to her chest and blew out a breath. Hannah had called and texted a bazillion times, but Maddie ignored every attempt. She'd tossed and turned all night, trying to make sense of her BFF's ridiculous decision to move away.

The back door opened and Zak stuck his blond head out. "Wanna go for a run?"

It was the perfect day for a jog, not too hot with just a tiny bit of a breeze. She had to skate later and a cardio workout was usually a regular part of her Saturday routine. But she just didn't feel like it. "No, thanks."

"How about a smoothie? Mom got us a new Vitamix."

A smoothie? Tempting. "What kind?"

Zak stepped out on the porch and raised himself up to sit on the railing, facing her. "What kind would you like?"

Maddie shrugged. "Whatever you want is fine with me. No kale, though. Yuck."

"How long you planning to sit out here and feel sorry for yourself?"

"I'm not feeling sorry for myself."

"Really?" Zak gestured to the pile of Kleenex next to her. "I guess your allergies must be acting up again."

"Very funny. I'm still ticked at Hannah."

"Now we're getting somewhere." Zak said. "Maybe she'll change her mind."

"Doubt it. Her mom's got her convinced California's the best thing ever."

"Her mom's pretty over the top, isn't she?"

"I guess. I never really thought about it until now."

"She makes a hockey mom seem tame."

Maddie laughed. She could always count on Zak to cheer her up. While Nicholas was soft-spoken and studious—an "old soul" her parents called him—Zak was the life of the party. Apparently he was adorable, because her friends were always gushing about him. As a camp counselor at the YMCA's sleep away camp, he probably had all the middle school girls swooning over him.

"Maddie? Zak?" Mom came out on the porch. "Want to go meet the new neighbors?"

"Not really," Zak said. "We were going to make some smoothies and go for a run."

"You could run by their house," Mom slid onto the swing next to Maddie. "Dad saw the kids outside earlier and they've already got a new puppy."

"Wow. That was fast," Maddie said.

"We could jog by and say hello if they're out. Want to?" Zak asked.

Maddie shrugged. "I guess." It was better than sitting around, thinking about Hannah moving away. They still weren't speaking. Hannah had texted twice already today, but Maddie ignored her.

"Come on." Zak offered his hand and she grabbed it. He tugged her to her feet. "Meet you back in here in ten."

Maddie went inside and changed her clothes, her chest tightening just thinking about coming face to face with Sydney Gray. What are the chances? She couldn't wait to tell Hannah—*oh*. That's right. The days of telling Hannah everything were coming to an end.

Drawing a ragged breath, Maddie grabbed her shoes and padded downstairs. Zak was already outside, one hand on the porch railing as he stretched his quadriceps. She pulled the door open and sat down on the top step, slipping her feet into her shoes.

"How far do you want to run?" Zak asked, shaking out his legs.

"I'm supposed to do forty-five minutes of cardio and then I do thirty minutes of yoga on the Wii fit." Maddie tied her laces in a double knot.

"I'll pass on the yoga, but I think I can do forty-five."

"You're probably in great shape, running from all those middle school girls." Maddie stood up and winked.

Zak blushed. "I don't know what you're talking about."

"I'm sure you don't. Emily said you almost had to leave the theater last night when a bunch of them saw you." Maddie stretched her calves and then her hamstrings, while Zak pretended to text one of his friends.

"I'm sorry." He glanced up, feigning complete boredom. "Were you talking to me?"

"Don't deny it. I hear girls talking about you all the time."

"Whatevs. Are you about ready, smarty pants?" Zak slipped his phone into the armband wrapped around his upper arm.

"Let's go." Maddie led the way down the street, imagining all the things she'd say if she did see Sydney Gray. *Welcome to the neighborhood, please don't skate at my club. PHHS stinks. Seattle has great private schools. You should totally check those out.*

"Slow down, there, kiddo. We've got a long way to go," Zak jogged up beside her.

"Sorry. I like to run fast when I'm mad." She shortened her stride.

"What are you made about? Hannah?"

"That and the new neighbors."

"We haven't met them yet. What's up with that?"

"I'm convinced it's this girl from skate camp who totally intimidated me. She's seriously the best I've seen—not including the Olympics and stuff."

"So what if it is? There's room for more than one great skater around here." Zak nudged her with his elbow.

"No there isn't," Maddie growled. "Only three or four skaters qualify from the whole Northwest."

Fewer than that go on to Nationals."

"You'll just have to skate better than her, won't you?"

"Zak, it's not like—" Her words died on her lips as a raven-haired, blue-eyed boy stood in the new neighbor's yard, tossing a ball to a yellow lab puppy. Her heart thrummed in her chest and it wasn't from their workout. He was tall, with a light tan and broad shoulders. He wore a Seattle Sounders jersey, neon green shorts and black Adidas soccer shoes.

He looked up and waved. "Hey."

Maddie stopped running. She was speechless. She licked her lips but no sound came out.

Zak glanced at her but kept jogging toward the boy. "Hey. I'm Zak Boone, this is my sister, Maddie. We heard you were new to the neighborhood."

"Dylan Gray," he said, bumping Zak's extended fist. "Nice to meet you."

"Is that your puppy?" Maddie asked. *Duh, Mads. Real cool.*

"That's Lila Jane. We just got her. Want to play?" Dylan handed Maddie the ball. She forced herself to make eye contact. His teeth were sparkling white as he offered a small smile. Her heart leaped into her throat. The air between them practically crackled with electricity. He was about the hottest thing to move into Magnolia Ridge in quite a while.

"Sure." She tossed the ball for the golden ball of fuzz and Lila chased it down, tail flitting back and forth as she retrieved it and dropped it at Maddie's feet. "Wait until Emily finds out about you."

"Is that your dog? Emily?" Dylan asked.

"No," Maddie glanced at Zak. "Emily's our little sister. She loves animals."

"She's always wanted to be a veterinarian. Right now she and Maddie run a pet-sitting service."

"Oh, yeah. My parents mentioned something about that." Dylan rubbed the back of his neck. "You guys go to Preston Heights?"

"I do. Maddie will be a freshman." Zak winked at Maddie. She went back to throwing the ball for Lila Jane, grateful for the distraction. She could feel Dylan's eyes on her, making her blush. Hopefully he wouldn't notice. Zak, either.

"How's the soccer team?" Dylan asked.

"Pretty good." Zak linked his arms over his chest. "I'm more of a hockey guy, but I think the soccer team went to state last year. There's lots of club soccer around here, too."

"A hockey player, huh? I should introduce you to my sister. She's a figure skater."

Maddie froze. "What's her name?"

"Sydney Gray. Ever heard of her?"

Maddie's heart pounded in her chest. *I knew it.* "I think I saw her at camp. I'm a skater, too."

Dylan's eyes lit up. "Really? She just got back from camp, right before we moved. Boy, she is not happy about leaving her club."

"I bet." Maddie rubbed the soft downy fur on Lila Jane's belly, wracking her brain for something kind to say about Sydney. But all she could think about was the murmurs of appreciation from the people in the stands when Sydney landed yet another incredible jump in front of all the skaters and coaches.

"You're pretty good with that puppy. Maybe you and your sister should come by more often," Dylan said.

Maddie's stomach vaulted into a series of backflips. She swallowed hard. "Um, sure. Don't you think you should ask your parents?"

Dylan glanced back at the house. "I would, but they took my twin sister over to check out the ice rink. Emerald skate? Emerald ice?" He shrugged. "I can't remember what it's called."

"Emerald City Skate Club," Maddie murmured.

Dylan snapped his fingers. "Yeah, that's it. So you've heard of it?"

She nodded. "That's where I skate."

"Well, you'll definitely have to come back by and meet her then. She'll be excited to have another skater in the neighborhood."

*Doubt it.* Sydney hadn't exactly given anybody the warm fuzzies at camp. She kept to herself, face to her phone and ear buds jammed in her ears most of the time. A few of the younger girls coaxed a smile out of her, but she gave everyone else the cold shoulder.

"Mads?" Zak nudged her shoulder. "Did you hear what he said?"

Maddie pasted on a smile. "Yeah, sure. Sounds great. Emily and I will come by tomorrow and say hello."

"Looking forward to it." Dylan smiled and bumped fists with Zak again. "Nice to meet you. Thanks for saying hi."

Maddie managed a wave then followed Zak back down the driveway and through the neighborhood. First Hannah decides to move away and now she'd probably have to watch Sydney Gray demonstrate her perfect short program every single day from now until Thanksgiving. Her stomach clenched. Only four skaters advanced from regionals. How could she move on to sectionals if she had to out-skate Sydney Gray? What an epic disaster.

# CHAPTER 5

*Pro: Max says healthy competition only makes you better.*
*Con: Is the competition still healthy if she's your new teammate and determined to dominate?*

"I can't believe you're going to let her try out. That's not fair." Maddie fisted her hands on her hips and glared at Max. Mom would come unglued if she heard her talking to her coach like that, but she couldn't stand by and let Sydney Gray waltz right in and take over ECSC.

Max pinched the bridge of his nose between his fingers. "Maddie, calm down. Sydney's a talented skater. But nothing's been decided yet."

"What about the other skaters you turned away?" Maddie grasped for anything that might convince Max to change his mind. "None of them get a special tryout."

Max put his hand on her shoulder. "Want to tell me what's really bothering you?"

Maddie huffed out a breath. "I'll never make it past regionals if she skates here."

"Doing well at regionals is based on your talents and abilities. Not those of the other skaters."

"But I watched her at camp, Max. She's so awesome. We'll never—"

"That's enough, Maddie. Healthy competition only makes you

better. Let's skate, shall we?"

Maddie clamped her mouth shut and nodded. This conversation was obviously over. She pulled her inhaler from her bag and took a puff, drawing the medication into her lungs. After a few seconds, she blew out a slow breath. She drank a few sips of water, then tugged off her skate guards and stepped on the ice.

Emily and her best friend Katelyn Montgomery were already warming up, although they were doing more giggling and chatting than skating.

"Hey, Mads. What's up?" Taylor Quirk leaned against the boards, twisting an elastic band around her mass of long strawberry-blond curls.

"Hi, Taylor. Ready for school on Tuesday?" Maddie skated in wide figure eights, waiting for her friend to join her. Taylor went to one of Seattle's elite private schools. They'd both skated at ECSC since they were little girls.

"I guess. I can't believe summer's almost over." Taylor skated to catch up with Maddie. Maddie didn't want to think about it. Starting her Freshman year was going to be stressful enough, especially without Hannah.

"Did you hear about Hannah?"

Taylor nodded. "She posted on Facebook. Totally bummed."

Maddie stroked her blades against the ice, picking up speed. "Have you talked to her?"

"I sent her a text but she didn't answer. It's like she's already gone. I'm sorry, Mads. This stinks."

Maddie shrugged. "I'll get over it. It's not like I can change her mind."

"It's the worst news ever." Taylor shook her head as they rounded the corner of the rink and skated back toward Max.

"Wait. There's more," Maddie said. "Sydney Gray is going to try out here."

Taylor snowplowed to a stop. She narrowed her eyes and stared at Maddie. "You're kidding."

"True story. Ask Max." Maddie waved as Alyssa stepped on the ice and began warming up.

Taylor glanced at Max but he held up his hands. "Not now. I know what you are going to say. No more. We're here to skate. Let's go."

Maddie groaned inwardly and took another lap, skating in tandem with Taylor. The sound of their blades carving into the ice soothed her anxious thoughts. Maybe Sydney would hate it here and beg her parents to go back to Colorado. But that meant Dylan would go, too. Her cheeks warmed at the thought of him. She'd never seen eyes that blue, or hair that—

"Maddie," Max called from across the ice. "Let's start with combo spins today. I want to see a camel-layback-sit, with or without a spread eagle. Your choice."

"Got it." There wasn't a spread eagle in either her short program or her long, but she knew better than to argue. Max was already annoyed with her line of questioning about Sydney. He was right. It was time to focus.

Maddie mentally played the music for her short program in her head, grateful for Elise and her excellent choreography skills. She loved the thrill and excitement of a great jump, but the artistic elements of spinning well were just as fun to practice. The footwork leading into her spins was sure to gain the judges' favor in competitions. Skating in a wide arc, Maddie went around Alyssa, who was practicing her double Axel. She rotated her hips out, feeling the stretch in her leg muscles. Spreading her arms, she tipped her chin and glided sideways across the ice in a flawless spread eagle. The air was cool on her face and a section of her ponytail blew across her face, but she didn't care. This is what she loved about skating.

"Great hip rotation, Maddie," Elise called from across the ice.

Maddie smiled. While she still had plenty of speed, she lifted her left leg quickly and leaned forward until her torso was parallel with the ice, spinning in four quick revolutions. She transitioned into a layback, spinning even faster, with her head dropped back and arms hugging her torso, leg flying closer to the ice to keep her momentum going.

Fixing her eyes on the rafters of the rink, she gritted her teeth against the dizziness and spun faster. After six revolutions, the burning in her quadriceps reminded her it was time to change legs, the hardest part of the combination spin. Dropping her left leg to the ice, she dug in with her edge, propped her hands on her thigh and spun eight more times. Coming out of her sit spin, she skated a few strokes and finished with a flourish of both arms.

"Well done." Max and Elise both applauded from their place at the boards.

Alyssa and Taylor skated over and offered high fives. "The best combo spin ever," Alyssa said, her blue eyes sparkling as her palm connected with Maddie's.

Warmth flooded through her. "Thanks, you guys. You're the best."

*Bring it on, Sydney Gray.* Maddie skated over to get another sip of water.

Her enthusiasm was short-lived. The doors to the rink opened, letting a stream of sunshine spill across the concrete floor. Sydney Gray stepped in, her black hair twisted into a bun, high on top of her head. She had on a red tank top that emphasized her lean, spindly arms. Black leggings completed her practice attire, while she carried her white figure skates in one hand. The woman with her was tall and willowy, wearing a long, flowing turquoise-blue tunic over white skinny jeans. They walked up to the boards, Sydney's expression very stoic as she glanced around at the other skaters. It was quiet as they all stared and Maddie could hear Mrs. Gray's shoes scuffing on the concrete. Maddie's pulse sped up. This was not happening.

"Ladies, say hello to Sydney Gray and her mother, Mrs. Gray." Elise instructed the girls while beckoning for Sydney and her mother to join them. "Consider this your official welcome to Emerald City Skate Club."

Mrs. Gray smiled brightly but Sydney just stood at the boards, head held high. She had the same startling blue eyes as her twin brother, but possessed none of his friendliness.

*Oh brother.* Maddie exchanged a meaningful glance with Taylor.

*Won't this be fun?*

"Sydney, once you're warmed up, we'll start with a game of Simon Says. For lack of a better phrase, it's sort of an icebreaker."

All the girls groaned at Max's terrible pun and went back to skating. Maddie tried not to stare as Sydney laced up her skates. She practiced her spread eagle at the far end of the rink, wondering what kind of elements Max would ask her to demonstrate for a tryout. Sydney stepped onto the ice and began skating. She still hadn't said a word to anyone. After several laps, she stopped in front of Max, her blades kicking up a small pile of ice flakes. "I'm ready."

"Okay, then. Alyssa, why don't you start us off?"

Alyssa smiled at Sydney and brushed a hand through her short, pixie style haircut. "Simon says, show me a toe loop."

Katelyn and Emily stood off to the side and clapped while the older girls skated across the ice. Everyone landed their toe loops effortlessly.

"Maddie," Max said. "Show us what you've got."

Maddie swallowed hard. The whole point of Simon Says skater-style was to demonstrate a move that nobody else could emulate. Her chest tightened. What could she possibly do that Sydney hadn't already mastered?

"Um, Simon Says, show me a quadruple Lutz." Maddie pushed off, skating backward several strokes before using her toe pick to launch from the outside edge of her right foot, willed her body to spin four times in the air in opposite direction. She landed on her left foot with only a slight wobble. Whoa. That was close. She glanced at the other skaters. Alyssa was getting up off the ice. That meant they were down to three.

"Taylor, your turn."

Taylor skated across the ice, her pale blue t-shirt billowing out behind her. "Simon Says show me your best double axel."

Not a problem. Maddie and Sydney were at opposite ends of the rink and Maddie nailed hers. She could tell by the murmurs from the rest of the girls that Taylor and Sydney had landed theirs, too.

"Sydney? Why don't you be Simon?" Elise said.

Maddie groaned inwardly. Not fair. She licked her lips in anticipation of what Sydney might call out.

Sydney skated in a wide arc, hands on her hips. "Simon says show me a triple Salchow."

Maddie's heart lurched. She could do it, but it wouldn't be pretty. Max and Elise said she needed to work it into one of her programs, but it had always been one of the toughest jumps for her to master.

Of course, Sydney showed them all exactly how it was done. She was all grace and elegance as she skated across the ice, vaulted into the air from her inside edge, spun effortlessly through the air four times before landing like a raindrop on a leaf—on her opposite leg, of course.

Maddie's pulse sped up. She picked up speed as she skated across the ice. Her effort was doomed from the beginning. Whether it was from intimidation or fatigue, Maddie lacked the power she needed and couldn't spin more than twice. Flustered, she landed on the same leg she took off from—a huge deduction if this were an official competition. Cheeks flaming, she skated back toward the others lined up along the boards. Alyssa and Taylor offered sympathetic smiles but Maddie fought back tears.

"Looks like Sydney is the winner of that round. Congratulations, Sydney."

"Thanks." Sydney flashed Maddie a rare smile and Maddie couldn't ignore the triumphant look in her eyes.

"That's all for today, ladies. See you Monday," Max said.

"Come on, Mads. Let's go do some retail therapy," Taylor said, patting her on the shoulder.

"I can't. Emily and I have pets to take care of." She didn't usually pass up shopping, especially on a Saturday night. But Maddie wanted to get away from the rink as soon as possible. After being one-upped like that, she wasn't in the mood for a trip to the mall.

# CHAPTER 6

*Pro: Pet sitting is a great excuse to run into the cute new neighbor.*
*Con: Too bad it runs the risk of seeing your new rival, too.*

"C'mon, Maddie. I want to go see that new puppy. Do you think we can stay and play?" Emily twisted a lock of her long blond hair around her finger, knee bouncing incessantly while she waited for Maddie to finish her cereal and her banana. Mom would be down in a minute to start working on their traditional Sunday morning brunch, but Maddie couldn't wait that long. She was starving.

"I don't know, Em. Are you sure this can't wait until later?"

"No. We'll be at the pool later. Besides, don't you want to see that cute guy again?"

Maddie spooned the last of her cereal into her mouth. "Who said he was cute?"

"I saw your text message to Alyssa."

"What?" Maddie glared at her little sister. "Since when do you read my texts?"

"Since you left your phone lying on the counter while you were in the shower." Emily wiggled her eyebrows.

"Stay away from my phone, all right?" Maddie rolled her eyes, pressing her lips into a thin line to hide her smile. She snatched her phone off the counter and shoved it in the back pocket of her shorts.

Tossing her banana peel in the trash, she put her cereal bowl in the sink. "Let's do this thing."

"Mom said we should take them these cookies." Emily slid a white cardboard box wrapped in a black-and-white polka-dot ribbon off the counter. "Besides, I thought you liked puppies?"

"I do. I just don't want to run into Sydney Gray." Maddie pulled open the front door and bounded down the front steps.

"Sydney Gray? The skater?" Emily slammed the door, her flip flops slapping against the steps as she hustled after Maddie. "Where is she?"

Maddie rolled her eyes. "Have you been paying any attention to what's going on? The Grays are the new family in the neighborhood, the same people that have the puppy you can't wait to see."

"Okay, okay. You don't have to bite my head off."

Maddie sighed. "I'm sorry. You're right. I'm just super stressed, that's all."

"But what if she's really nice?" Emily asked. "She might be your new BFF."

"Doubt it. Didn't you see her at the rink? She hardly said a word."

"Maybe she was scared." Emily kicked at a pebble and sent it bouncing across the street.

"Whatever." Maddie huffed out a breath. Sydney didn't look scared. She looked perfectly calm. Confident. Especially when she landed that Triple Salchow without even a hint of a wobble.

They walked along in silence. Mostly silent, anyway. Emily hummed a little song—sounded like Katy Perry's "Roar." Maddie wished she could absorb some of Emily's attitude. She didn't seem to have a care in the world.

"Let's stop by the Connors and make sure their bearded dragon has enough crickets," Emily said, pointing to the Connors house three doors down.

"Ew." Maddie cringed. "So disgusting. You go ahead. I'll wait out here."

"Not fair." Emily stopped at the bottom of the Connors driveway. "Half of everything, remember? Our jobs are supposed to be equal."

"I'll feed the Magnani's cats and change the litter box if you get the crickets. How's that?"

"Deal. Hold these. I'll be right back." Emily handed Maddie the box of cookies then jogged up the driveway. She fished a spare key out of the frog dish by the front steps and let herself inside the Connors' house.

Maddie shifted the cookies to one hand and pulled out her phone and checked her messages. Hannah had stopped texting her. Good. It was easier that way. She brushed aside the twinge of disappointment that lodged in her chest. The truth was, she'd thought about calling Hannah at least five times last night. Hannah would totally get why Maddie was flipping out about Sydney skating at ECSC. But Maddie wasn't going to give in. Hannah should be chasing her, not the other way around. No. She'd wait until it was time to say goodbye.

"They're good." Emily popped back through the front door, turning to check the lock behind her.

"Cool." Maddie tucked her phone back in her pocket and they crossed the street to the Magnani's house. She scooped up the bundled newspaper from the driveway and pulled Saturday's mail from the box.

"Have fun," Emily said, giving Maddie a little wave with her fingers.

"Thanks. I'm having a blast already." Maddie knew she'd probably regret her end of the deal. The Magnani's cats were notorious for leaving a mess in their owners' absence. Punching the access code into the keypad by the garage, Maddie waited while the door hummed and clicked, holding her breath in anticipation of what might be waiting for her. The door rolled up to reveal the empty garage. Phew. No dead trophy rodents. Since the cats could go in and out the pet door through the back door in the garage, there was usually a dead mouse or the occasional bird proudly displayed in the middle of the garage floor or on the steps leading into the house.

Maddie put the newspaper and mail in the bin by the steps and made short work of changing the litter box, wrinkling her nose at the foul odor. This was not her idea of a good time. But she thought about the new custom-made costume for regionals she'd be able to buy with the money she and Emily earned. At least that made the task more palatable. She dumped out their water bowls in the utility sink next to the hot water heater and added plenty of fresh water. The cats had yet to make an appearance. Scooping a healthy serving of food into each of their bowls, Maddie hurried out of the garage and punched the code in again to let the door roll back down.

"That wasn't so bad, was it?" Emily asked.

"I guess not. It's definitely easier when they don't leave any dead animals lying around."

"Did you know that's a sign of ..."

While Emily launched into a long explanation about cats and their motivations, Maddie watched a Volvo station wagon pull out of the Gray's driveway three doors down. Were they leaving? Maybe she and Emily would have to stop by another time. But then the front door opened and Mrs. Gray stepped out on the porch, Lila Jane tucked under one arm.

"Oh, hello," she called to them. "You must be the Boone girls?"

Emily practically sprinted up the driveway. "I'm Emily. That's Maddie. Cute puppy. This is Lila Jane, right?"

Mrs. Gray smiled and her arm full of bangle bracelets jangled as she set Lila Jane in Emily's open arms. "Here. You look as if you need your puppy fix this morning."

Maddie hung back, clutching the box of cookies to her chest. She cut a quick glance to the open door behind her. Was Sydney home? What about Dylan? She touched her hand to her hair, wishing she'd taken the time to blow it out before she rushed out of the house.

"Nice to see you again, Maddie. We didn't get to talk much at the rink yesterday. How long have you been skating?"

Maddie swallowed hard. "Since I was little. Second grade, I guess."

"How about you, Emily?"

Emily looked up from where she sat cross-legged on the lawn with the puppy. "This is my fourth year. I'm only at juvenile now."

"That's something to be proud of. I'm sure it took a lot of hard work to get where you are."

Emily dipped her head and went back to rubbing Lila Jane's head.

Maddie inched further up the driveway and held out the cookies. "These are for you from our family. Welcome to Magnolia Ridge." She hated how robotic her voice sounded. Mom would not be impressed.

"Oh, thank you. You didn't have to do that. Would you girls like to come in? Lila Jane can come with you." Mrs. Gray took the box of cookies and motioned for the girls to come with her, the hem of her chevron-striped maxi dress swooshing around her bare ankles.

Maddie and Emily looked at each other. A few minutes couldn't hurt. Emily didn't look as though she was willing to leave that puppy anytime soon. "I guess for a few minutes. We have to be home for brunch in a little bit."

"How nice. My husband took Dylan to Starbucks to get some breakfast. They're so excited to have Starbucks so close here. You just missed Sydney. She's on a trail run."

So they weren't home. Maddie followed Mrs. Gray into their house. "On a Sunday? We usually take Sundays off."

Mrs. Gray paused to pull some of Lila Jane's toys out of a shoe box next to her crate in the kitchen. "Well, Sydney is very driven. She doesn't usually take a day off. Dylan wants to stay in shape in case he gets to play soccer."

Max and Elise would not be happy if they found out about one of their skaters doing extra workouts. A lecture would certainly follow about the importance of rest, allowing muscles to repair and rejuvenate so they could perform well.

"She's so adorable," Emily squealed as she started a game of tug-o-war with the puppy and her rainbow-colored rope.

Maddie looked around for a place to sit. Moving boxes were stacked two and three high around the kitchen and family room, some opened and some not. One full of trophies and medals sat nearby and Maddie tried to ignore it. Those were probably all of Sydney's figure skating awards. Several tunics and blouses were draped over the back of the kitchen chairs, most with the tags still on.

"I like these shirts." Maddie touched the sleeve of a royal blue shirt that reminded her of something Mom would like to wear.

"Oh, thanks." Mrs. Gray re-folded the newspaper, clearing a space at the kitchen table. "I do some design work on the side. Those are from a place I used to own in Denver. I'm hoping to open a clothing boutique at some point."

Maddie glanced at a stack of picture frames sitting on the table. The top picture was of the Gray family standing at the edge of the rink, Sydney smiling as she held up a medal draped around her neck and a bouquet of roses tucked in the crook of her very lean arm. Maddie couldn't help but wonder why they really left Colorado. The Northwest Pacific region had some great skaters, but not as many as Colorado and California. Did Sydney convince her family to move to a place where she could win easily? *Stop.*

"Did you move here for Mr. Gray's job?" Emily asked, right on cue.

"Yes. He starts at Microsoft on Monday." Mrs. Gray continued to move around the room, unwrapping the paper from the items she pulled out of a cardboard box.

"Have you found a veterinarian for Lila Jane yet?" Maddie shifted from one foot to the other, half-wishing Dylan would come back from Starbucks yet also hoping that he didn't.

"No, we haven't. Sydney found an ad for puppies on Craigslist as soon as we drove into town. I wasn't planning on getting her so soon, but this is a big move and whatever makes things easier for Syd—"

"Lots of families around here use Magnolia Animal Hospital. It's close by," Emily explained, picking up Lila Jane and rubbing her cheek against the puppy's side. Lila Jane squirmed in her arms, her pink tongue lavishly spreading kisses of gratitude in return.

"Do you work there?" Mrs. Gray asked.

Maddie smiled. The perfect segue to launch into their pet-sitting spiel.

"No, I'd like to. But I can't skate and have a regular job. That's why we have our pet-sitting service. Right, Mads?"

"That's right. For a small fee, we provide regular walks, cuddles, food, and water as needed. For puppies, we can come by as often as you need. Obviously that would be in the morning and afternoon, with school starting and everything."

"Wow, that's quite a sales pitch you have there." Mrs. Gray linked her arms across her chest. "Any references I should contact?"

"You can ask anyone on this street. We've probably worked for all of them," Maddie said.

"Except for Mrs. Baxter at the end. She's never had pets and doesn't let anyone touch her plants and flowers," Emily explained.

Mrs. Gray laughed. "Sounds fastidious. Let me talk to my husband and get back to you."

The front door opened and Maddie turned to see Dylan and the same man who talked to the movers come inside, a cardboard carton full of Starbucks cups in their hands. Her pulse sped up as her eyes met Dylan.

"Hi," he said, stopping when he recognized her.

"Hi," Maddie whispered, feeling her cheeks warm under his piercing blue gaze.

"Honey, this is Maddie and Emily Boone from down the street. They skate at the same club Sydney checked out yesterday," Mrs. Gray said.

"Hi, ladies." Mr. Gray offered a hand to Maddie. "Nice to meet you."

Maddie shook his huge hand and smiled. He wore a green plaid button down over khaki cargo shorts, with brown Keen sandals. He looked as if he'd stepped straight out of the pages of REI. Definitely fit right in around here. "Nice to meet you, too, Mr. Gray."

"Is Sydney back yet?" He looked around. "She'll be sorry she missed you."

Maddie bit her lip and shrugged. She could still feel Dylan watching her.

"She usually runs for a couple of hours, Dad." Dylan brushed past Maddie and set the coffee carrier on the kitchen table.

Yeah, Max would definitely have something to say about that. Maddie cleared her throat. "Did you talk to the soccer coach yet?"

"Would you like some coffee?" he asked at the same time. "You can have Sydney's. She never drinks it—"

"Dyl." Mrs. Gray shot him a warning look. "You can't give away your sister's coffee."

"It will be cold by the time she gets back," Dylan insisted. "She won't drink it, anyway." Mrs. Gray pasted on a smile for Maddie. "Don't mind him. Can I get you girls something to drink?"

This was awkward. "Um, no. We really need to get going. C'mon, Em."

"Not yet, Mads. I need to give this girl some love. Yes I do," Emily crooned as Lila Jane toppled over, chasing a ball.

"Thanks for asking about soccer," Dylan said, twisting his cup in the cardboard sleeve. "I have a meeting with the coach before school on Tuesday."

"I hope it works out. I heard one of our best players transferred," Maddie explained, forcing herself to maintain eye contact and hoping he couldn't hear how loud her heart was hammering in her chest.

"Yeah, I heard that, too." Dylan drank some more coffee, rocking back on his heels.

"Em, we really need to get going," Maddie prompted.

"Okay, okay." Emily got to her feet. "Hey, we're all heading to the pool later. You all should come check it out."

*No. No. No.* Sometimes she wished Emily wasn't quite so friendly.

"That sounds fun," Dylan said. "Are you going, Maddie?"

Maddie could only nod.

"Is it the one in the neighborhood?" Mrs. Gray asked. "I think I drove by it yesterday."

"Yep, just a couple blocks from here. It's so fun. You'll love it," Emily said.

Yeah. So fun. Maddie did not want to spend her afternoon at the pool with Sydney. All week at school and at the rink was going to be bad enough.

"Maybe we'll see you there," Mr. Gray said, walking with them to the front door. "Thanks for stopping by."

"Bye," Maddie managed a quick wave in Dylan's general direction.

Once the door swung closed behind them and they were out on the sidewalk, Maddie nudged her sister with her elbow. "Thanks a lot. Why did you invite them to the pool?"

Emily stared at her with wide eyes. "I thought you said he was cute. Why wouldn't you want him at the pool?"

"Because that means he'll bring his twin sister, too. Duh."

"Maybe she won't come."

"Whatever. I bet she will. She'll probably look perfect in her teeny tiny swimsuit, too."

"Boy, what has gotten into you?"

Sydney Gray, that's what. Of all the neighborhoods in Seattle, why did they have to move into this one?

# CHAPTER 7

*Pro: What could be so bad about one last day at the pool?*
*Con: It's all fun and games until Sydney steals the show ... again.*

"Brunch is ready," Mom said, sliding a ham and cheese quiche onto the dining room table.

Maddie's mouth watered. She slid into her chair and reached for the juice pitcher. This was her one day to indulge in a great meal, without worrying about calories or how she'd look in costume.

Emily sat down across from her. "I invited the Grays to the pool, Mom."

Maddie glared over the top of her juice glass.

"Maddie is so happy about it, too." Emily winked and popped a bite of cantaloupe into her mouth.

Mom grabbed a spatula for the cinnamon rolls, eyes darting between both girls. "What's the matter with inviting the Grays?"

"It's bad enough she has to skate with us. I'm just not crazy about her living down the street and hanging out with us at the pool, okay?"

Zak came and sat down. "Her brother seems cool."

Emily arched one eyebrow. "See?"

Maddie squirmed in her seat, the tips of her ears growing warm. She had a new two-piece swimsuit that she bought for the summer and hadn't had much time to wear, even though Alyssa and Taylor said she totally rocked it. But with Dylan around, now she wasn't so sure. Swimming was not her favorite thing, either.

"Your ears are red, what's up with that?" Zak sat down next to her.

"Nothing."

Dad came in and took his place at the head of the table. "How are the neighborhood pets, ladies?"

"All good." Emily dug into her slice of quiche. "The bearded dragons ate four crickets. Crazy, right?"

Maddie cringed. "Gross."

"We stopped by the Grays. Their puppy is adorbs," Emily said.

"Anything else adorbs at the Gray's house, Mads?" Zak asked.

"Shut it," Maddie growled. "I don't know what you're talking about."

Dad's blue eyes twinkled. "Something cute live there besides the puppy?"

"Maddie thinks Dylan Gray is nice to look at." Emily giggled.

"You two are so lame." Maddie took a bite of cantaloupe and pretended not to care about her family's good-natured ribbing.

"Isn't that ironic?" Mom slid into her chair. "Your toughest competition comes with an adorable twin brother?"

It was ironic, all right.

*******************

Maddie spread her turquoise beach towel with purple polka dots across the deck chair next to the pool. She stripped her cover-up off and tossed it into her bag, carefully adjusting the straps on her purple bikini. The sun was warm on her skin and she was glad she remembered to put sunscreen on before she left the house.

Someone cannonballed into the pool, splattering drops of water across the deck. Several girls squealed and somebody turned up the music. Maroon 5's "Love Somebody" blared through the speakers mounted on the light posts that stood around the pool. Maddie took a sip of her water then leaned back in her chair, reaching for the latest copy of InStyle magazine. A perfect Sunday afternoon.

"Hey, Maddie. Can I sit here?" Maddie lifted her sunglasses and glanced at Delaney Wheeler, one of her neighbors and classmates since Kindergarten.

"Hey, Delaney. Go ahead. Emily's in the pool with Katelyn."

"Thanks." Delaney shimmied out of her own cover-up to reveal an emerald green bikini. "I love your suit. Where'd you get it?"

"Nordstrom. Does it look okay?" Delaney hesitated.

"You look great," Maddie reassured her. "I haven't seen you this summer. What have you been up to?"

"I made the cheerleading squad, did I tell you that?" Delaney smiled proudly.

"I saw it on Facebook. Congratulations."

"Thanks. We work out a lot, do fundraisers and stuff. We just went to camp a few weeks ago. It's been crazy."

"I bet. When's the first home football game?" Maddie asked. She hardly ever had time to watch other people's sports, but maybe she'd be able to squeeze in a game or two this fall.

"I think—whoa. Who the heck is that?" Delaney's hand froze in mid-air, her mouth falling open.

Maddie looked across the pool to where the Gray family was making an entrance. Sydney led the way, wearing quite possibly the smallest red bikini Maddie had ever seen. Dylan followed behind her, looking pretty incredible in royal blue board shorts with huge white flowers all over them. "That would be the Gray family. Our new neighbors."

"Could that bikini get any smaller?" Delaney whispered.

"I don't know. I'm distracted by her twin brother. That's Dylan, by the way."

"Are they going to Preston Heights?"

"As far as I know. Sophomores, I think." Maddie pretended to study her magazine but watched from the corner of her eye as the

Grays picked out four chairs together at the far end of the pool. Sydney dragged her chair under the nearest umbrella.

"Is he trying out for football?" Delaney continued to pepper her with questions.

"He's into soccer. She's a figure skater." A bead of sweat trickled down Maddie's spine. It was hotter than she thought out here. She reached for her water bottle and took another sip.

"She's so … lean. And tall. I didn't know skaters could be so tall." Delaney sprayed sunscreen all over her legs and arms.

Maddie felt her perfect afternoon slipping away. She did not want to sit here and talk about Sydney all afternoon. Maybe they could just look at Dylan instead.

"Look, here comes Hannah. Is it true she's moving?" Delaney asked.

Maddie's heart lurched. "Hannah? Where?"

"Right there. She's coming this way." Delaney tilted her head toward the entrance again.

Maddie thought about jumping in the pool or making a run to the snack stand. But Hannah had already spotted her and was crossing the pool deck. She stopped in front of Maddie's chair, casting a shadow across the magazine in her lap.

"Maddie?" Hannah shifted her tote bag from one shoulder to the other. "Can I talk to you for a second?"

Maddie shrugged. "I guess so."

"I think I'll leave you two alone for a few minutes." Delaney scooted off her chair and went toward the snack stand. Maddie secretly wished she'd gone with her.

Hannah sank down on the empty seat to Maddie's left. "Say something. Please."

Maddie's stomach clenched. "What do you want me to say, Hannah? You're moving away. All because of skating."

"I'm really sorry. I'd be bummed, too, if it was you."

"Then why don't you stay?" Hot tears pricked her eyelids. Maddie hated that her voice quavered.

"I can't. My parents really want me to go. I don't want to let them down."

"You're the one who has to skate, not them." Didn't Hannah see how crazy this was?

Hannah sighed and looked out over the pool, her slender shoulders slumped. "Can we try to have fun while I'm still here?"

"Don't you start school soon?"

"Mom's going to homeschool me. We started already but we're not leaving until Saturday."

"Homeschool?" Maddie lowered her sunglasses and looked at her friend over the frames. "Are you serious?"

"Lots of skaters do it," Hannah said.

"I know. But I never thought you'd be one of those skaters." Maddie pushed her glasses back up over her eyes and looked away so Hannah couldn't see the tears that threatened to fall.

"It's not like I'm gone forever. I'll come back to visit. We'll see each other at regionals, sectionals … maybe nationals."

Maddie drew a ragged breath and blew it out slowly. "I guess I can't stay mad at you forever. Besides I can't wait to tell you about the girl who's trying out at the rink."

A wide smile spread over Hannah's face, her teeth white against her milky complexion. She jumped up and threw her arms around Maddie's neck. "Thank you for saying that. I don't know what I'd do without your friendship."

Maddie hugged her back. "Now sit down. I have to tell you what happened."

Hannah crisscrossed her legs and rested her chin on her hand. "So who tried out? One of the girls from Magnolia's rink?"

"Nope." Maddie leaned closer. "Sydney Gray?"

Maddie's brown eyes were wide as saucers. "*The* Sydney Gray? From skate camp?"

"Yes, and keep your voice down because she's sitting right over there. Don't look, she's watching us right now."

Hannah froze. "What do you mean 'don't look'? She's seriously right behind me?"

"Why? Were you going to ask for her autograph?" Maddie asked.

"No way. She wouldn't speak to me at camp. I don't know why today would be any different. Are Max and Elise going to let her join the club?"

"Probably. She blew us all out of the water yesterday." Maddie gnawed on her lower lip. "What am I going to do, Hannah?"

"You're going to keep being the awesome skater that you are. Don't worry about her. Besides, I watched her at camp, she looks like she's sick or something," Hannah whispered.

"I know, right? We stopped by to say hello to her this morning and she was on a two-hour run. Max would flip if he knew that."

"I don't want to turn around and stare at her but maybe she's anorexic or something?"

Maddie saw Dylan coming straight toward them. "Shh. Here comes her twin brother."

"Hey, Maddie." Dylan stopped near the end of her chair, hands on his hips. For the second time today, Maddie was grateful she could keep her eyes hidden behind her shades so he wouldn't catch her staring at his tan, buff chest. Her mouth felt dry. She licked her lips quickly.

"Dylan, this is my friend, Hannah. Hannah, this is Dylan Gray."

"Nice to meet you," he waved to Hannah and then looked back at Maddie. "Zak and I are going to ride the lazy river. Want to join us?"

"Sure. Want to come, Hannah?" Maddie got to her feet, suddenly very self-conscious in her swimsuit in front of Dylan. Guys were so lucky. They just threw on a pair of swim trunks and called it good.

Hannah smiled. "Sounds like fun. I can't pass up a chance to harass Zak."

They followed Dylan over to the line for the lazy river. Maddie tried to play it cool while Hannah walked behind him, waggling her eyebrows and nudging Maddie with her elbow. Maddie glared daggers at her friend, but could barely suppress a giggle. *Stop it.*

"Sydney doesn't want to come along?" Maddie asked.

Dylan shrugged. "I offered. She's too busy messing with her phone and reading her magazines."

Zak joined them in line, immediately pulling Hannah's head under his arm and rubbing his knuckles on her hair. "What's up with the move, short stuff? Nobody said you could do that."

Hannah squealed and tried to break free. As an only child, and an adopted child at that, she didn't get to experience the joy of having older brothers. Nicholas and Zak had done their part to play pranks, tease and generally make Hannah feel like one of the family. Hannah pretended to hate it, but Maddie knew she enjoyed the attention.

"I'm trying to get away from you, Zak Attack." Hannah managed to get out from under Zak's arm and slugged him playfully in the shoulder.

"Where is she moving to?" Dylan asked.

"California. To work with another coach," Maddie said, twisting her lips into a frown.

"That stinks. Are you pretty good friends?" They were at the front of the line and Dylan let her climb into the first inner tube, then secured one for himself.

"We've been friends a long time, skating together and everything. I'm sad she's leaving, but I get it." Maddie sank into the bright yellow tube, letting her arms and legs hang over the edge. She trailed her fingers through the cool water as she started to float slowly down the man-made river.

"Moving sucks." Dylan's leg brushed against hers as his inner tube collided gently with hers. Maddie felt a tingle of excitement shoot down her spine. She was at the pool, hanging out like a normal teenager with the hottest guy around. *Somebody pinch me.*

"Preston Heights is pretty cool. Seattle has a great vibe, too. What was your favorite thing about Colorado?"

"The weather. We had a lot more sunshine than Washington does. I'm not looking forward to all this rain I keep hearing about." Dylan nudged the wall with his toe, sending his inner tube into a slow spin.

"At least you don't have to shovel it." Maddie grimaced. The ice rink was cold enough, she couldn't imagine having to shovel their driveway all the time. Seattle practically shut down when it snowed more than an inch.

Hannah and Zak floated up beside them and they rafted their inner tubes, floating the rest of the way down the river in a cluster. Maddie tipped her head back and let the sun warm her face. She could definitely get used to this.

When they got to the end of the ride, the lifeguard asked them to give up their tubes because a long line had formed. Maddie climbed out and almost collided with Sydney, who was waiting next to the lifeguard tower.

"Hey, Syd." Dylan hoisted himself out of the water, little droplets falling off of him and landing on the concrete. "What's up?"

"There's a volleyball game getting started over on the sand courts. Will you play with me?"

"Just you and me or what?" Dylan tipped his head toward Maddie, Zak and Hannah.

"If I find one more, we could play three on three," Zak suggested.

Maddie wanted to kick him. Who wanted to ruin a perfectly awesome afternoon with a game of volleyball? Yuck.

Sydney narrowed her eyes, considering his suggestion. "I'll be on your team. Can you find a third? We could play against Dylan, Maddie and her friend."

Despite the warm sunshine, Maddie felt the hair on the back of her neck stand up. Was everything a competition with Sydney?

"I don't know," Hannah said. "If I get hurt playing volleyball, my—"

"We'll go easy on you, Hannah," Zak said. "Promise."

*Doubt it.* Maddie bit back a snide reply. She hadn't played volleyball in quite a while but maybe it could be fun. She'd get to spend a little more time with Hannah and Dylan.

While Zak grabbed one of his buddies from the pool to come and play, the rest of them walked over to the volleyball court. The net rippled in the light breeze. Sydney scooped up the volleyball lying in the sand and bumped it to her twin. Dylan set it into the air just above the net where Sydney swooped down and spiked it into the sand on the other side.

Oh boy. Hannah and Maddie exchanged nervous glances.

"Nice hit, Syd." Dylan ducked under the net and jogged over to retrieve the ball. Sydney tossed her long black ponytail over her shoulder and stretched her arm muscles.

Zak came back to the court with Delaney trailing behind. "Hey, Sydney and Dylan, this is Delaney. She's a friend of Maddie's and a cheerleader at Preston Heights."

"Hi, guys," Delaney grinned and gave a cute little wave.

"Nice to meet you," Dylan said.

"Hi," Sydney said, pulling her left foot backward to stretch her quadriceps.

Maddie stifled a laugh. She was really taking this seriously. "I think you're on their team, Delaney."

"Cool." Delaney shrugged and took her place on the other side of the net with Sydney and Zak.

Dylan, Maddie and Hannah formed a tight triangle in the back court. "Watch out for Sydney. She likes to drop her serve right over the edge of the net. It's hard to return."

"Looks like spiking's her thing, too," Hannah whispered.

"Don't worry about that, I can probably block it." Dylan put his hand palm down in the middle of their mini-huddle. "On three, we yell 'teamwork' okay?"

Maddie put her hand on top of his, enjoying the contact, even if it was only for a second. Hannah piled both of her hands on top.

"One, two, three …"

"Teamwork!" They yelled and broke apart.

Several kids from school had left the deck and wandered over to the volleyball court. They stood in little clusters, discussing the odds of who might win this game. A couple of them had their phones and were already snapping pictures. Maddie tried to ignore the wave of uncertainty that washed over her. Her less than stellar performance would probably be a Vine video in a couple of minutes. *Great.*

"You guys can serve first," Sydney said.

"Can't argue with that." Dylan jogged to the end of the court and stepped over the yellow ribbon staked in the sand and marked the boundaries. He tossed the ball in the air and fired a serve deep into the other side of the court. Delaney bumped it to Zak, who set it to Sydney.

Maddie knew from the minute the ball left Zak's fingertips that she was in trouble. The gleam in Sydney's eye mixed with her vertical jump when she left the sand should have been the warning signs she needed to defend herself. Before she could put her hands up in defense, the ball hurled straight at her, hitting Maddie in the eye with a sickening smack.

Hannah gasped and the crowd of onlookers went silent. Maddie yelped and fell to the sand, clutching her face. The sting was worse than any botched landing on the ice.

Dylan kneeled beside her in the sand. He touched her shoulder. "Maddie? Are you okay?"

Maddie shook her head, afraid to speak. Spots dotted her vision. Her eye was already tearing up but she refused to give Sydney the satisfaction of seeing her cry.

"I think someone went to get some ice from the snack bar. Can you see anything, Mads?" Zak was at her side now.

She pulled her hand away and blinked several times. Hannah came into focus. "I-I think so."

"Wow," Dylan said, studying her closely. "I bet that hurt."

"Yeah," Maddie whispered.

"Syd? You have anything you want to say?"

Sydney stood on the other side of the net, hands on her hips. She shrugged. "Sorry."

Dylan's expression hardened. He looked at Maddie again, his blue eyes filled with concern. "Don't worry about her. She takes everything a little too seriously."

"I heard that." Sydney kicked sand at her twin brother. "It's our serve, by the way. One nothing. You guys need a sub?"

A surge of anger coursed through Maddie's veins. Could she be any more obnoxious? It was going to be a long season on the ice.

# CHAPTER 8

*Pro: A chance to take cross-train in Pilates class might be one benefit of a black eye.*
*Con: Unless you spend the whole time worrying about how you'll look on the first day of school.*

Maddie stepped onto the elliptical machine at the Preston Heights Athletic Club and punched the button for an interval workout. The flat screen television mounted from the ceiling in front of them showed an early morning talk show, highlighting the latest news for Labor Day. Mom selected her own workout, the machine beeping to life as she picked up speed.

"How's your face?" Mom asked.

"It's a little sore." They usually jogged together on Monday mornings, but Maddie couldn't stand the pounding of her shoes on the indoor track. It made her face absolutely throb. So she was playing it safe and cross-training on the elliptical.

"I'm just glad nothing's broken," Mom said, flipping through the pages of a home-decorating magazine propped on the front of her machine. "A broken nose would make it hard to skate."

Maddie cringed. Hockey players skated all the time with broken noses. It was probably a badge of honor, but she couldn't imagine skating with one. "I wish I didn't have to start school with a black eye.

So embarrassing."

"It's not too bad," Mom said. "With a little makeup and a bright colored shirt, you'll be good to go."

"That's going to take a lot of makeup, Mom. I have a huge shiner."

"I wouldn't call it huge," Mom insisted.

"It covers most of my cheek. That's huge." The machine's intensity kicked in and Maddie grabbed the handrails as she pumped her legs to keep up. Images of the volleyball coming straight at her, coupled with Sydney's satisfied expression, brought a fresh wave of anger. "I can't believe Sydney did that. After we welcomed them to the neighborhood, invited them to the pool—"

"I doubt she did it on purpose, honey. It's just a game."

"That's the thing," Maddie huffed. "It isn't just a game with her. She has to be the best. Every time."

"You just met her? How do you know?"

"Mom, you can ask anybody that was there. She asked us to play, she picked the teams and then intentionally spiked the ball at my face." Her chest started to tighten but Maddie ignored it and pumped her legs harder. A tough workout was exactly what she needed right now. How could Mom take Sydney's side in all of this?

"Maddie, calm down. Maybe she thought playing volleyball would be a good way to get to know you and your friends."

"I cannot believe you are defending her." Maddie breathed in through her nose and out through her mouth, trying to quell the familiar struggle to gain air. Where was her inhaler, anyway?

"I think you did the right thing inviting them to the pool and being kind, even when she's not being especially friendly," Mom said, watching the television as the weather person showed the local forecast.

Maddie's machine eased up, shifting to an easier interval. Maddie took a sip of water from her bottle in the cup holder, hoping that would help her feel better.

"I'm sure it's hard for Sydney, and for Dylan, too. Maybe you and the other girls could invite Sydney to do something fun that doesn't involve sports. Like the mall or—"

"Sydney probably doesn't go to the mall. She's too busy running," Maddie growled. Her vision started to tunnel and Maddie instantly regretted her snide comment.

"Exercise does seem like it's pretty important to her." Mom glanced her way. "Maddie, are you feeling okay?"

Maddie tried to relax and take slow, even breaths but she started to panic. That strange wheezing sound was coming from her. She pointed to her chest and hit the emergency stop on the elliptical.

"Maddie, where's your inhaler?" Mom jumped off her own machine and looked around. Then she started yanking things out of her purse.

*Please hurry.* Maddie propped her hands on her head and paced in a circle, the resistance in her chest growing stronger.

"Here." Mom held out her rescue inhaler. "Take a puff."

Maddie shook the inhaler, popped off the cap and sucked in the medication. She held it in as long as she could, then took a second puff. Immediately, the tightness released and she sucked in two deep breaths. The panic subsided and the dizziness melted away.

"How about some water?" Mom held out Maddie's water bottle.

Maddie took a few sips and put then twisted the cap back on. "I think I can finish my workout."

"No way," Mom said, shaking her head. You are not getting back on that elliptical."

"Mom, I can't quit after just ten minutes. We're supposed to do two workouts on Mondays."

Mom glanced at the clock. "There's a Pilates class starting at seven. How about that?"

Maddie nodded. "All right."

Mom wiped down their machines with an antibacterial wipe and tossed it in the trash. Then she collected their stuff and led the way down the hall to the rooms where group exercise classes were held.

Taylor and her older sister Mia were waiting beside the door, along with a few other women.

"Hi, Mads." Taylor offered a sympathetic smile. "I'm sorry about your face."

"Is it bad?" Maddie asked.

Taylor hesitated.

Maddie slumped against the wall. "I knew it. Who starts their freshman year with a ginormous shiner?"

"A little makeup and you'll be good to go," Mia said.

"See?" Mom grinned triumphantly. "Mia's right."

"I heard Sydney spiked the ball right at your face. The Vine video showed the whole—"

Maddie gingerly covered her face with her hands. "Great, I'm on Vine. I knew this would happen."

"Don't worry about it. Everyone will have forgotten by tomorrow," Taylor said.

"Yeah, right. Not when they see my eye and people are whispering and pointing," Maddie wailed.

"Relax, Mads," Mia said. "Someone will drop their tray at lunch or get their books knocked out of their hands by a Senior before the second bell. You'll be old news by tomorrow afternoon."

"Listen to Mia. She survived high school," Mom said.

Mia not only survived but had been the Valedictorian of the senior class last spring. She was off to Stanford along with Nicholas in a couple of weeks. Maddie knew Mia was right but that wasn't helping her feel better now. Stupid Sydney.

The instructor came to the door, all fit and bubbly. "Good morning," she said, keys jangling as she unlocked the door and flipped on the lights inside.

"Good morning," they said, filing in behind her. Maddie and Mom had to borrow mats, while Mia and Taylor spread their own out in the middle of the floor.

"Okay, class. I'm Tessa, your instructor this morning. Let's get started with our hundreds."

Maddie mirrored the instructor's movements by lying flat on her back on the mat. Pushing aside her anger and frustration toward Sydney, she tried to focus on getting a great workout. Max and Elise were always talking about how much a strong core would improve her skating, especially the height on her jumps. Besides, she read in Skating magazine that all the elite skaters were doing Pilates now.

"Lift your legs, and bend your knees. We call this the table top. We're keeping our backs flat, aren't we? Then lift your head and shoulders, using that strong core. Now hold."

Maddie complied, feeling the burn in her abdomen.

"This is called the scoop, because we want those deep abdominal muscles working hard. Now lift your arms, keeping your elbows locked and press down. Pretend like you're smacking the water in the pool. Smack, smack, smack. Very good!"

The pool sounds pretty good right about now. Holy moly.

"Breathing is very important. We don't hold our breath in Pilates, do we? No. Breathe out for five smacks, then breathe in for five smacks. Great job."

*One two three four five.* Maddie counted in her head, pressing her lower back into the mat as she struggled to keep her head and shoulders lifted.

"Now this is called the hundreds, because we'll do one hundred smacks before we're finished here. You'll be tempted to rock as you get tired, but don't rock."

Maddie wanted to quit after a few cycles but she pressed on, visualizing her body flying through the air in an effortless triple-triple. *Smack, smack, smack, smack, smack.*

"Who can tell me one of the six principles we keep in mind when we're doing our Pilates workouts?" Tessa asked.

"Concentration," Mia called out.

"Very good. Concentrate on those arm pumps, engaging your deep abs and keeping those shoulders lifted nice and high. We're halfway to one hundred. Keep going."

"This is intense," Taylor said, grunting. "I know, right?" Maddie squeezed her eyes against the burn and pumped her arms some more.

"If you're up for a challenge, straighten your legs toward the ceiling," Tessa said.

No way. Maddie normally didn't shy away from a challenge but that was asking a lot. Her stomach was on fire. She kept her legs right where they were.

"Okay, we're on our last cycle. Count it out with me. Five-four-three-two-one. Relax."

"Whew." Maddie fell back on the mat and filled her lungs with air. She released the air, feeling the burn in her abs slowly subside.

"Okay, now we'll move on to our next exercise," Tess said. "This is one of my favorites called the single straight-leg stretch."

Maddie finished the rest of the class, pushing herself to do her best and test the limits of her endurance. Tessa was an upbeat but demanding instructor. Maddie wanted to give up halfway through, but she hung in there. By the end, she felt more confident, knowing she was one step closer to pursuing her dream of qualifying for sectionals.

# CHAPTER 9

*Pro: Skating competitions on your home ice are a huge advantage.*
*Con: Unless you crack under pressure and totally blow it.*

"Ladies, gather around and listen to a few announcements, then we'll get started." Max motioned for the skaters to circle up at center ice. Maddie glided to a stop next to Elise, avoiding eye contact with Sydney. They hadn't said a word to each other since they both stepped on the ice to warm up.

"I know you're focused on school starting soon, but it's competition time and we need to start thinking about hosting regionals in October, right here on our home ice." Max paused for dramatic effect.

The girls clapped and cheered. Skating at home, sleeping in your own bed before a competition and not dealing with the hassles of travel were all huge advantages. Max and Elise, as well as the other skate clubs in the Seattle area, had worked hard to earn the opportunity to host this year.

"First, we need to get ready for Spokane. That's our only competition before regionals and the Lilac Skate club always produces some talented skaters," Elise added.

"We'll spend the next few weeks polishing your programs and talking about what we'd like to see you accomplish in Spokane, keeping in mind the bigger competition scene of regionals and for some of you, sectionals after that."

Butterflies took flight in Maddie's stomach. How she wanted that statement to apply to her. She'd do whatever it took to skate her best at regionals and advance to sectionals. Maybe if she worked hard enough, she could even make it to Nationals in Omaha in January.

"We'd like to officially welcome Sydney Gray to Emerald City Skate Club," Max said, smiling and swooping his arm in Sydney's direction.

The other skaters offered polite applause but Maddie couldn't ignore the subtle glances in her direction. Between Vine, Facebook, and Instagram, probably all of Seattle had seen a picture and/or a video of Sydney's spike and Maddie's now-blackened eye.

Maddie tipped her chin and forced a polite smile, even managed to clap along with the other girls. This club was big enough for two elite skaters, right?

"Maddie, let's work on that triple-triple today, okay?" Elise skated alongside Maddie.

Maddie nodded. "Sounds good."

Normally Elise was busy keeping her kids occupied while Max did most of the hands-on coaching. Their kids must have been with their grandparents or maybe a babysitter today, because they weren't hanging around the rink. Maddie appreciated Elise's positive approach and strategy for mastering an element on the ice. Max knew the intricacies of all the elements like the back of his hand, but Elise was better at breaking them down into more manageable chunks.

"Why don't you skate a lap and then give it a go?" Elise peeled off and turned in a slow circle, waiting for Maddie to make her first attempt.

Maddie skated around the rink, trying not to notice how Max had gone right toward Sydney and was engrossed in conversation with her already. Maybe that's why Elise was working with her today. *Don't think about it. Focus.*

The rink was smooth as glass today, freshly glazed by the Zamboni before the girls started skating. Her blades glided across the ice and she gained momentum, rounding the curve to skate back toward Elise.

Turning around, she skated backward on her left leg, leaning on her back outside edge while lifting her right skate to plant her toe pick into the ice. Spreading her arms wide, she used all her momentum to jump straight up, remembering to rotate in the opposite direction. *Hips. Shoulders.* She tucked her arms across her chest as she spun three times in the air, touching down on the edge of her right skate. Swinging her left leg around, she went right into the triple toe by digging her toe pick in again and rotating the other way. But she lacked the energy she needed to complete three full rotations and stepped out of the jump early, wobbling as her right outside edge touched the ice. Flustered, she didn't even try the third element of the complex combo. She puffed her lips and blew out a breath, skating in a wide arc around Elise.

"Very nice entry into that triple Lutz, Maddie." Elise clapped her hands. "Great arms, nice and tight rotation in the air."

"But I couldn't finish the triple toe, not to mention the triple loop." Maddie tucked a loose strand of hair behind her ear and glanced across the ice at Max and Sydney. He had his back to her. Good thing. She didn't want him to know she'd botched that combo. Again.

"I think we should focus on what you are doing well for now. Let's take it back to the Lutz on its own. You've mastered that. Let's skate that a few times instead of working so hard to land the whole combo all at once."

"But I want the points of the whole combo. If I don't practice it, I'll never land it."

"If you master the nuances of the individual components, you'll boost your confidence. That's what we need right now, is a confident Maddie." Elise skated beside her, patting Maddie's shoulder.

"I know I can do the whole thing, Elise."

"I know you can, too. We'll get you on the pole harness soon and Max can work with you to make little adjustments. Then your jumps will be even better."

"I don't know why I can't get it," Maddie whispered. So frustrating. She watched as Sydney and Taylor landed perfect triple Axels at the opposite end of the ice. Max whooped and hollered for both of them.

Sydney didn't express any emotion, but Taylor pumped her fist in the air and high-fived Max. Maddie turned and skated the other way. She was thankful for coaches who were supportive and encouraging, cheered them on when they did well. But skating was so competitive and she felt so frustrated that she couldn't master this tricky combination.

"You could always change it up a bit, make the third element a triple flip," Elise suggested.

"No." Maddie shook her head. "I can get this. I don't want to change it."

"I know you don't. It was just a suggestion. Think about it."

Maddie looped back around the rink, crossing one skate behind the other to gain as much speed as possible. *You can do this.* Flipping around, she skated backward, leaning forward to gather as much power as possible before she planted her toe pick. Vaulting upward with a grunt, she knew she was in trouble before she even finished her second revolution. Something didn't feel right. Her blades tangled up like they were magnetically attracted to one another and she fell to the ice, landing so hard on her bottom that the bruise on her face throbbed.

She sat there for a minute, elbows on her knees, head in her hands. This stinks.

"Momentum, Maddie." Elise skated up beside her and snowplowed to a stop. "You have to have tremendous speed going into that jump, otherwise you're toast."

Sydney picked that exact moment to land a beautiful triple combo right in front of her. Maddie bit her lip hard and looked away. Momentum. Right. She felt as though hers had been swiped away the minute Sydney Gray stepped on Maddie's home ice.

\* \* \* \* \* \* \* \* \* \* \* \* \* \* \* \* \* \* \* \*

Zak's red Toyota Camry sat at the curb, engine purring. Maddie could see Nicholas riding shot gun. Emily jogged ahead, blond hair streaming behind her and duffle bag bouncing against her shoulders. Maddie couldn't jog right now, even if her life depended on it. Between the Pilates workout and all that jumping, she was absolutely worn out.

Maddie climbed in the back seat beside Emily and buckled up. Nicholas turned around and handed her an iced coffee from Starbucks. "A little post practice pick me up." His deep voice echoed through the car.

"Wow, thanks." Maddie pressed the straw to her lips and sucked in a mouthful of cold, sugary sweet vanilla latte. "Are you sure you have to leave for college?"

"Hey, what about me?" Emily asked.

"I've got a strawberry frap for you, little sis." Nicholas passed the pink and white drink through the space between the front seats.

"Awesome. Thanks, Nick." Emily's eyes lit up as she cupped her hands around the plastic cup.

"You're welcome."

"Good practice?" Zak glanced over his shoulder before shifting the car into gear.

"Yep," Emily said.

"No," Maddie said.

"Wow, that good, huh? What happened?" Nicholas asked.

"Stupid triple combo jumps. I'll never get it." Maddie stared out the window and took another drink of her coffee.

"That's what you said about the double Axel," Nick reminded her.

"And the Salchow, and the Lutz," Zak said.

Emily couldn't help but smile. They were right. She'd whined a lot about messing those up, too. Now she could do a Salchow practically in her sleep. Well, not quite. But it wasn't as hard as it used to be.

"We're headed to Target for last minute school stuff," Zak said. "Do you want to come with us or go home?"

"I'll stop by and check on Lila Jane," Maddie said.

"No fair," Emily protested.

"You need school supplies, girlfriend," Maddie said. "I got my stuff before I went to camp."

"Boo." Emily sipped on her Frappuccino and stared out the window.

As they drove into their neighborhood, Maddie could see Dylan outside on his lawn, playing with Lila Jane. Zak must have noticed, too, because he slowed the car to a stop at the end of the Gray's driveway.

"Oh, Lila Jane," Emily crooned.

"School supplies, remember?" Zak said. "Want to get out here, Maddie?"

Maddie felt Dylan's eyes on her through the window. "Zak, what are you doing?" she hissed.

"You said you wanted to check on the puppy. So here you go. Check." He glanced over his shoulder and waggled his eyebrows.

Shoot. So he did know she thought Dylan was hot. Busted. "I guess I'll walk home then. Thanks for the ride." She climbed out of the car and slammed the door, but not before she heard Zak and Nicholas making kissing noises and high-fiving each other. They were so immature sometimes.

Dylan waved as she shouldered her duffle bag and walked up his driveway. She racked her brain for something cute to say, but nothing came to mind. She cleared her throat. "Hey. How's Lila Jane?"

"Good. How's your eye?" He winced as he glanced in her direction.

"Is it that bad?" She touched her hand to her cheek. All that drama at the rink over her jumps made her forget about the bruising on her face.

"It's not too bad. I'm just sorry it happened. I don't know what Syd was thinking."

*I do.* Maddie let the silence hang between them. She'd thought and said enough snotty things about Sydney in the past twenty-four hours. Bashing her to her twin brother was not cool. Lila Jane scampered over, her tail wagging happily as she sniffed at Maddie's tennis shoes.

"She likes you," Dylan said.

Maddie leaned over to pet the puppy's head, receiving several sweet kisses in return. "That's good. I like her, too. Em's so bummed she can't stop by and play. My brothers are taking her to get the rest of her school supplies."

"I did that today, too." Dylan tossed the ball in the grass and Lila Jane went after it.

"Did you meet the soccer coach?"

"Yep. I worked out with them this morning. You're looking at the newest member of the Preston Heights Viking soccer team." Dylan thumped his chest proudly.

"Congratulations." Maddie smiled. "I bet you'll have a great season."

"Will you come watch me play?" he asked.

Maddie's skin warmed under his direct stare and even more direct question. She swallowed hard and nodded. "Of course. I mean, when I can. With skating and all—yes. I'll be there."

A wide grin stretched across his face. "Sweet. Thanks."

Now that she'd promised something she'd have a hard time achieving, she hurried to change the subject. "Are you ready for tomorrow?"

He shrugged. "I guess. Not crazy about starting at a new school, but I hope soccer will make it worth it."

"There's some good guys in your class. I'm not just saying that because one of them is Zak, either."

"He is pretty cool. Who was that riding with him?"

"Today?" Maddie thought for a second, taking one last sip of her iced coffee. "Oh, that's my oldest brother, Nicholas. You probably won't see much of him. He's leaving for his freshman year at Stanford pretty soon."

"Stanford? Wow."

"He wants to be a doctor, like our dad."

"Good for him." Dylan glanced back at the house and then at her. "Thanks for stopping by, Maddie. I hope your eye feels better."

"Thanks. You're welcome." She closed her eyes and cringed. *Dork.* She opened her eyes and walked backward down the driveway. "Good luck tomorrow."

"Yeah, you too."

Maddie hurried home, thinking about those blue eyes and that dark hair. Not to mention he'd invited her to watch his soccer games. She didn't know how she'd pull that off, with skating and chores and probably homework, too. She was jogging up the steps when she realized she hadn't seen Sydney anywhere. Was she still at the rink?

Maddie pushed open the front door and heard her phone chiming with a text. Dropping her bag on the floor, she pawed through it until she found her phone. It was a text from Hannah.

Mom bought our plane tickets. We're leaving Wednesday. Can you come over?

Maddie slumped against the door, her heart in her throat. She tossed her phone back in her bag. It was too soon.

*******************

Maddie sat in the car in front of Hannah's house, gnawing on her thumbnail. She stared at the front door. This was awful. If she'd known Mrs. Springer was going to book an earlier flight, she'd—

"C'mon, sweetheart." Mom reached over and squeezed Maddie's leg. "Waiting isn't going to make this any easier."

"I can't do this," Maddie whispered.

"I think we should make this quick. Maybe a couple of pictures, some hugs and then we go. The longer you hang around, the harder it will be."

"A few minutes? That's all?"

"Trust me. It will be easier for everyone." Mom unbuckled her seat belt and climbed out of the car. Maddie swallowed hard and slid out from the passenger side.

Hannah opened the front door before they could ring the doorbell. She was wearing jeans and a purple Washington Huskies t-shirt. Maddie wondered who Dr. Springer would take to games now that he wouldn't have Hannah around. How sad was that?

"Hey, Mads," Hannah whispered, her cheeks damp with tears.

"Hey." Maddie tried to smile but failed miserably. She felt her lower lip tremble.

Mrs. Springer came out of the kitchen with her camera and her phone, smiling brightly. "Hi, girls. How about some pictures?"

Maddie and Hannah made their way into the family room and automatically posed in front of the fireplace. They'd stood here dozens of times over the years and posed for pictures: before competitions, during sleepovers, just messing around on a rare night with nothing else to do. They stood arm in arm and faced the cameras, but Maddie couldn't muster a genuine smile.

"Girls, you can do better than that." Mrs. Springer switched from her phone to her camera. Maddie wanted to beg her one last time to change her mind, but she knew it wouldn't do any good.

"How about one silly one?" Mrs. Boone suggested.

Hannah and Maddie managed their cheesiest smiles, posing as if this was an ordinary Labor day and they'd be friends forever, skating at the rink the next afternoon.

But it wasn't an ordinary night. They had to say goodbye. No matter how many times they texted or Skyped or whatever, things wouldn't be the same. Ever. Hannah walked with her back to the front door while their mothers tried to find something to talk about.

"Thanks for coming over," Maddie said.

"You're welcome." Maddie stared at the floor, unable to meet Hannah's gaze.

"Give me hugs." Hannah flung her arms around Maddie's neck. Maddie patted her back, the tears flowing freely now.

Hannah pulled away, swiping at her face with the back of her hand. "I'll miss you."

Maddie could only nod, dragging her fingers under her eyes. This was horrible.

She opened the front door and jogged to the car, climbing inside and tugging her knees up under her chin. Mom climbed in and started the engine.

"I'm proud of you, honey. I need you to buckle up so we can go."

Maddie dropped her feet to the floor and yanked the seat belt across her body. Hannah and her mother stood on the porch, waving. Maddie managed a small wave in return before they drove away, her chest aching. How was she ever going to survive freshman year without her BFF?

# CHAPTER 10

*Pro: A new year, new school, and a new opportunity.*
*Con: It's hard to make new friends when everyone seems to know where they fit.*

Maddie's eyes popped open at five a.m., just like always. She was about to get up and pull on her practice clothes when she remembered she didn't have an early morning rink session. Today was the first day of freshman year. Max and Elise had waived their morning session since everyone would be a bundle of nerves and too distracted to practice well, anyway.

After a shower, Maddie wiped the condensation from the bathroom mirror and examined her eye more closely. The purple parts of the bruise were starting to fade into greenish-yellow. Gross. It wasn't as bad as she thought, but still a miserable way to start the school year. Especially high school. She picked out some white shorts and her new royal blue shirt with the shoulders cut out. After the perfect blowout and using the flat iron, her hair was exactly how she wanted it.

"Mads, out of the bathroom." Emily pounded on the door. "It's my turn."

Maddie sighed. "All right, all right. Just a sec." She gathered up her makeup bag and opened the door. She padded into her parent's room but the bed was empty. Dad had probably left for rounds at the hospital and Mom was working on their traditional first day of school breakfast: stuffed French toast.

Standing at her parent's bathroom counter, Maddie proceeded to conceal the bruising on her face with a liberal dose of makeup. After brushing, swabbing and dusting concealer, bronzer and powder all over her face, she finished with eye shadow and lip gloss. There. Dozens of skating competitions had given her plenty of practice in applying her makeup to hide almost anything. She turned one way and then the other, giving herself one last examination. Satisfied, she headed downstairs for breakfast.

Zak was already at the table, drinking a smoothie and messing around with his phone. Mom was in yoga pants and a long t-shirt, a baseball cap concealing her hair. She carried a plate of bacon to the table.

"Good morning," Maddie said, reaching for a juice glass in the cabinet.

"Good morning, sweetie. You look nice," Mom said.

"Thanks."

Zak grunted, obviously his usual cheerful early morning self.

"Can I have a ride to school, Zak?" Maddie sat down at the table with her juice.

"Uh huh."

Mom brought the stuffed French toast to the table and a few cartons of yogurt. Maddie plated her food, allowing herself a couple slices of bacon and a small portion of French toast. It might be tradition, but she didn't need to blow all her hard work at the gym and on the ice. Especially if she only had one workout today.

Emily came downstairs later, all dressed and ready for school. She chattered about her friends, the new fifth grade teacher at her school, if Lila Jane would be okay without anyone checking on her all day. Maddie smiled. What Zak lacked in enthusiasm about a new day, Emily more than made up for.

He perked up by the time they climbed in his car.

"Ready for the seniors to stuff you in your locker?" He asked, slamming his car door and sliding the key into the ignition.

"Very funny." Maddie tucked her backpack between her knees and clicked her seat belt into place.

"Watch out for the lunch table trick. That's the worst." Zak shook his head.

"What's the lunch table trick?" Maddie's stomach swirled with anxiety.

"Where you sit at the only empty seat at a table in the cafeteria. Then right when you start to eat, everybody gets up and moves. Girls do it all the time. So mean."

"I'll try to remember that," Maddie said. Geez Louise. Like she needed another thing to worry about. Between finding her way around the massive high school, trying to adjust to seven new teachers and figure out who her friends were, now she had to add pranks from the upperclassmen to her list. Hello, high school.

They rode the rest of the way with the radio cranked, Mumford and Sons singing their current hit. Cars were pouring into the student parking lot and Zak squeezed into the last remaining space in a crowded row. He walked with her to the front steps of the school then gave her an affectionate punch in the arm.

"Knock 'em dead, sis. If anybody gives you grief, text me." Zak winked and took the concrete stairs two at a time.

Maddie swallowed hard and pasted on a smile. A dull ache settled in her chest. She wasn't supposed to be standing here alone. She and Hannah had talked about this day all summer, planned out exactly how it was going to go.

Butterflies crashing against her ribcage, she double-checked the outside pocket of her backpack for her inhaler. But this wasn't an asthma attack. It was just plain old nerves.

*You can do this.* Drawing in a deep breath, she shouldered her backpack again and climbed the steps. Inside the front doors, the hallways were crowded. She was glad she'd taken extra time with her appearance. Preston Heights kids had money; that much was obvious. From Juicy Couture sweatpants to Joe's jeans and even a few Prada handbags, Maddie made a mental note to step up her game when it came to choosing her outfits for school. *Wonder what Mom will have to say about that.*

Moving toward the hallway where most freshmen had their assigned lockers, she recognized Dylan standing with a few guys from the soccer team. She expected him to ignore her but he surprised her with a wave and a tip of his chin.

"Hi," she said, smiling as she walked by.

A few of the guys stopped talking for a second then a chorus of "whoas" and "Dylan, who's the girl?" followed her. She was glad they couldn't see the red splotches that were probably breaking out on her neck right now. At least he had the courage to speak to her and cared enough to say hello. She'd probably be hearing about that later.

She navigated the crowd and found her locker, twisting the combination lock and opening the door. There were a few pictures in her backpack she wanted to put up, but that would have to wait. The bell was about to ring and she had a long walk to her first period English class.

A couple of girls she grew up with in the neighborhood had lockers near hers, but they were whispering and giggling as if they belonged together. Since they didn't skate she felt awkward trying to hang out with them. She walked past them on her way to English. She'd have to make friends other than Hannah somehow.

Maddie found her class in plenty of time and chose a seat right in the middle of the room. Mrs. Ackerman, the English teacher, was as intimidating as everyone said. She stood at a podium at the front of the classroom, several quotes Maddie didn't recognize scrawled on the white board behind her. Lots of kids were coming in and sitting down, talking about their summer vacation or how they'd spent the last long weekend of the summer. Maddie's plans included more skating and saying goodbye to her BFF. Yea.

Once Mrs. Ackerman passed out the syllabus, Maddie tucked it under her open notebook and let her mind wander. It wasn't that she didn't want to be a good student or couldn't focus, but when she was anxious, thinking about skating relaxed her. She was halfway through a rendering of her jump sequence in the margin of her notebook page when she felt several sets of eyes on her.

"Madison Boone?" Mrs. Ackerman was calling her name.

Maddie's head shot up. "It's Maddie, actually."

"Well, Maddie. Perhaps you could snap back to reality and tell us your thoughts on the summer reading requirement. I trust you read the Scarlet Letter?"

Maddie wanted to crawl under her desk. The girl across the aisle from her clapped her hand over her mouth, probably to keep from laughing. She had read it, but found the whole story to be maddening. The way they treated Hester was so unfair.

"I read it. I didn't think it was fair. The stuff they said and did to her."

Mrs. Ackerman arched one eyebrow. "Is that right? Perhaps you'd like to stop doodling and tell me more about that."

Maddie shrugged. "I don't really have much else to say."

"I see. Who can tell me some of the major themes in the novel? Other than fairness."

Maddie resisted the urge to doodle under Mrs. Ackerman's watchful eye and studied the syllabus instead.

The rest of her morning classes were pretty uneventful. After fourth period, she stuffed her notebook in her locker and walked alone to the cafeteria. Nicholas and Zak had always complained about the food but she thought the vegetable soup and the yogurt looked pretty safe. She put both, along with a banana and a cup of water on her tray and swiped her card through the card reader at the cashier's stand.

Glancing around for a place to sit, she heard Zak's warnings in her head. There was one seat at table where Delaney sat, but those were probably all cheerleaders and Maddie wasn't feeling that brave. She didn't see Zak around, but he wouldn't want to sit with her, anyway. She was about to grab the first empty seat she came to until she recognized Sydney sitting by herself. Gathering her courage, Maddie balanced her food on her tray and walked to where Sydney sat, pushing a salad around on her plate.

"Is anyone sitting here?" Maddie asked.

Sydney looked up, her fork halfway to her mouth. "No. Go ahead."

Maddie hesitated and then slid her tray onto the table. At least no one could jump up and leave them stranded. There wasn't anyone else around. She took a sip of water and tried to make eye contact. "How was your first morning?"

Sydney shrugged. "Fine."

*O-kay. This was like pulling teeth.* Maddie wished Dylan would show up, maybe he knew how to get his sister to talk. Or maybe she didn't talk to him, either.

"You aren't eating very much. Are you feeling okay? I mean, I know it's hard to eat when you're nervous. If you're nervous. You probably aren't all that worried about your first day of school—"

"I'm not eating because this food is crap. Not even the salad is edible," Sydney snapped.

Maddie stirred her soup, feeling ridiculous for talking so much. Why did she even bother? Sydney made it clear she didn't want to be friends.

"Why are you even talking to me, anyway?" Sydney glared at her. "I thought you were still ticked about your eye."

Maddie pressed her lips into a thin line. She was impossible. Why even bother? "I felt bad that you were sitting alone, that's all."

"I don't need anyone feeling sorry for me, okay? Thanks but no thanks." Sydney jumped up, grabbed her tray and dumped the salad in the nearest trash can. She jogged out of the cafeteria without looking back. Maddie watched her go, a heaviness settling over her. It was going to be a long year.

*******************

After school, Maddie was the first one to lace up her skates and step on the ice. Her friends and teammates, including Emily, were still in the locker room. Probably giving each other an instant replay of the day's events. *No thank you.* Maddie pushed off, her heart singing at the sound of her blades carving into the ice. So what if freshman year looked tough and Sydney stomped away from the lunch table? At least she still had skating.

Maddie skated two full laps, the stress of the first day of school melting away as she picked up speed. The ice was smooth as glass and Maddie couldn't resist the wide open space. She envisioned an arena packed with spectators, all watching in rapt attention as she took to the ice to skate her long program at the National Championships. *The Phantom of the Opera* played in her head as she flew across the ice, performing first a double axel and then moving straight into a triple toe loop. Adrenaline pumping through her, the crowd in her imagination applauded her perfect landing and the judges leaned forward with rapt attention, amazed by the beauty of her spread eagle as she glided past them. Smile. Always remember to smile. Maddie finished her impromptu performance by skating on her right leg, grabbing her left skate blade and tugging it up behind her head toward the ceiling. Ignoring the stretching sensation in her hip, she pushed herself to keep skating, spinning in four quick revolutions. Heart pounding, she came out of the spin with a quick jab of her toe pick into the ice and thrust her arms in the air. *Yes.*

"Nicely done, Maddie Boone, nicely done." Max stood at the boards, clapping loudly, a wide smile stretched across his face.

Maddie smiled, warmth flooding through her at his approval. She skated over and gave him a high five. Chest heaving, she reached for her water bottle and chugged several sips.

"I think that's the best Biellmann I've ever seen you skate. Where did that come from?"

Maddie shrugged. "I was just messing around, waiting for everybody else to come on the ice."

"Well, you should do that more often. That was excellent."

Maddie ducked her head and took another sip of water. But not before she noticed Sydney standing a few feet away, hands on her hips and eyes blazing as she watched the interaction between Maddie and

Max. *Whatever*. Maddie set her water back on the boards and turned away, buoyed by Max's encouraging words. This was going to be a great practice, she could feel it. If Sydney wanted to sulk because she had to share the limelight, that was her problem.

# CHAPTER 11

*Pro: A morning run in cool, fall weather complete with kisses and tail wags from a golden retriever ... the perfect start to a great day.*
*Con: Secrets and snide comments are never a good a combination.*

Maddie yawned and scooped her running shoes off the laundry room floor. The clock on the living room wall ticked toward six a.m. If they were going to get a run in before school and check on the Gambles' golden retriever, they'd better get going.

Emily stood at the counter, nibbling on a piece of toast. The first rays of early morning sun streamed through the window behind her, bathing the kitchen in a pale glow. This weather was too beautiful to ignore. There would be a lot of early morning workouts at the athletic club, once the rainy season hit. Maddie didn't want to waste an opportunity to run outside.

"Let's go, Em."

Emily nodded and put her plate in the sink. "Coming."

The morning outside was cool and refreshing, with a hint of fall in the air. In the distance, a lone boat motored across the lake, kicking up a white froth in its wake. Definitely the perfect morning for a run. Emily and Maddie stretched their leg muscles in silence on the front lawn.

"Ready?" Emily asked, jogging in place at the edge of the driveway.

Maddie nodded. They went left out of their driveway this time, reversing their usual route. The Gambles lived a good fifteen minutes away, marking the halfway point of their run. Dr. Gamble was an anesthesiologist at the hospital and always requested Emily and Maddie's pet-sitting services when he and his wife were out of town.

"Great job on the ice yesterday, Mads," Emily said, her long blond ponytail bouncing against her back as she ran.

"Thanks. I was just messing around." And trying to forget the stress of the first day of school.

"Whatevs. Nobody else can spin like that."

"I bet Sydney can," Maddie said, matching her stride with Emily's.

"I saw her giving you the evil eye. What's up with that?"

"Who knows?" Maddie's stomach clenched. Dylan was so friendly, not to mention a total hottie, but he'd probably never ask her out as long as Sydney was skating at ECSC. Sydney would freak if she knew Maddie even liked Dylan. *Liked Dylan.* Her cheeks warmed and it had nothing to do with jogging.

"Why is your face red already?" Maddie asked. "Did you forget your inhaler?"

"I don't need my inhaler," Maddie grumbled. To prove she was fine, she picked up the pace, challenging Emily to keep up with her.

"Take it easy. Spencer isn't that desperate to get outside, is he?"

The Gambles' dog, Spencer, was an older, adorable golden retriever. He didn't seem to mind being home alone, but he'd be overjoyed to see the girls when they got there.

"Spencer will be fine. I just want to get this over with." There was no way she'd tell Emily about her feelings for Dylan. They got along well, but Emily would have a ball with that juicy tidbit. She wouldn't be able to keep it to herself, either.

They ran the rest of the way to the Gambles' house without talking, the rolling hills in the neighborhood taking all their energy. Legs burning from the climb, they crested the last hill before starting down the other side. Dr. Gamble and his wife lived in a cul de sac at the bottom. Chests heaving, Emily and Maddie slowed to a walk in the driveway, hands on hips as they recovered. Spencer was already barking from inside the house.

Emily pulled a key from the pocket of her shorts and unlocked the side door leading into the garage. She re-emerged a few minutes later, Spencer's nails clicking on the pavement as he followed her outside. He trotted over to Maddie and slathered her outstretched hand with kisses.

"Hi, Spence." She rubbed behind both of his ears, smiling as his tail berated Emily's legs. Nothing like a friendly welcome from a golden retriever to start your day. They led him around to the fenced in backyard. Emily filled his water bowl while Maddie took his dish back to the garage to fill it with his dog food from the storage bin.

When she returned, Spencer nearly knocked her over in his eagerness to get at his breakfast. They waited while he practically inhaled his food, then took turns tossing the tennis ball across the backyard. He chased it down every single time, returning it to their feet.

"I'd stay here all day if I could, Spence." Emily patted his head while Maddie launched the ball one more time.

"We better go if we want to catch a ride with Zak," Maddie said.

They gave Spencer one last pat and made sure he was secure in the backyard with plenty of water and things to chew on. The hill looked daunting from where they stood, but Maddie thought about how high she could jump if her legs were strong and how much her endurance would improve if she kept up her cardio workouts the way Max wanted her to. She drew a deep breath and offered Emily a fist bump.

"Let's do this thing."

Emily bumped her fist against Maddie's and nodded. "I'm ready."

The first hill wasn't so bad and there was a flat stretch, a slight reprieve before they tackled the next one. Arms pumping, Maddie powered through the burn in her quadriceps and followed Emily to the top of the steepest hill in their neighborhood. Heart pounding in her chest, she stopped when they found Sydney at the top, doubled over on the sidewalk and clutching her lower leg.

"Sydney?" Emily reached her first, putting a hand on the back of Sydney's red nylon shirt. "Are you okay?"

"I'm fine." Sydney stood up, jaw clenched. "It's just a cramp."

Maddie kept her distance, biting on the inside of her cheek while Sydney tried to walk without limping. This didn't look good. Sydney tipped her head back and stared at the sky, shaking out her legs one at a time. Her arms were pencil thin, every muscle clearly defined as she fisted her hands on her hips.

"Do you want us to walk you home?" Emily asked, brow furrowed.

"I said I was fine, okay?" Sydney turned her back on them, but when she touched her foot to the pavement, she gasped and leaned over again, rubbing her lower leg.

"We can't just leave you out here, limping along by yourself," Maddie said.

"I know my way home. Go on, I'll be fine in a few minutes." Sydney rotated her ankle in a slow circle, avoiding eye contact.

"Then we're going to jog by your house and let your mom know you're out here," Maddie said.

Sydney's chin shot up, blue eyes flashing. "So now you're a tattle tale, too?"

Maddie winced and bit back a snide reply.

"Maddie's right," Emily said. "We can't leave you here. Walk with us."

It was a long, slow walk back to the Gray's house. No one said a single word. Emily fired several questioning glances her way, but Maddie silenced her with a pointed stare behind Sydney's back.

"Is your mom home?" Maddie asked as Sydney slowly limped up her own driveway.

"I don't know." Sydney climbed the steps without bothering to look back.

Emily tugged on Maddie's arm. "Let's just go. We're gonna be late for school."

Maddie's stomach clenched. She couldn't bring herself to just walk away. What if Sydney needed to see a doctor? Who would drive her to school? "I'm going to make sure somebody's inside. Just in case."

Emily huffed out a breath but followed Maddie up the steps and through the open door. Maddie side-stepped a discarded pile of packing material in the entry way and followed the voices toward the kitchen.

"Maybe you should—" Mr. Gray leaned against the counter, a coffee cup halfway to his mouth. He stopped talking when Maddie and Emily appeared in the kitchen. "Good morning, ladies. How can we help you?"

"We, um, wanted to make sure Sydney was okay," Maddie said. She cut a quick glance at Sydney, who filled a glass of water from the dispenser in the refrigerator door.

"Okay?" Mr. Gray's lips stretched into a thin smile over the rim of his coffee cup. "You're more than okay, aren't you, Syd?"

Sydney pressed the glass to her flushed cheek and nodded slowly. Maddie could feel the tension mounting in the room. Emily was right. Coming inside was a mistake.

"What about your leg?" Emily asked.

Mr. Gray's eyes narrowed. What's wrong with your leg?"

"Nothing." Sydney shrugged. "It's a little sore, that's all."

"You couldn't finish your run," Maddie said.

"It's hard to run hills when you're carting around that extra weight," Mr. Gray said. "Maybe lay off the ice cream before bed."

Emily sucked in a breath. Did he really just say that? Sydney drained her glass of water, her long black ponytail streaming down her back. Maddie wanted to turn and fly out the front door, but she felt like her shoes were filled with concrete.

Mr. Gray set his coffee cup in the sink and patted Sydney's shoulder. "Have a good day, sweetheart."

He walked past Emily and Maddie with a polite nod. "Ladies."

His shoes clicked across the hardwood and then the door to the garage opened and closed.

"Sydney—" Maddie moved toward her.

"You can go," Sydney said through clenched teeth. "I said I was fine."

"But—"

Sydney whirled around, eyes flashing. "Get out."

Maddie stepped back, startled by the angry outburst. She was only trying to help, to look out for her new teammate and Dylan's sister. Without another word, she nudged Emily toward the front door.

They slipped outside and were jogging again before they hit the street.

"Did he really call her fat?" Emily asked.

"Not exactly. Sort of." Maddie couldn't believe it, either. She wanted to pretend it hadn't even happened.

"She's not fat. I bet she doesn't even eat ice cream."

"Probably not." Anger surged through her. She'd heard about skaters who restricted calories and worked out too much, even skated with stress fractures. But not at their rink. If Max or Elise ever said anything like what they'd just heard, Mom and Dad would flip out.

"Are you going to tell Mom?" Emily asked.

"Tell her what?" They'd reached their own driveway and Maddie stopped running, resting her hands on her knees while she tried to catch her breath.

"About Sydney. Her leg and the stuff her dad said."

Maddie straightened, grabbing her foot and pulling it up behind her so she could stretch her leg. "No way. She doesn't want our help."

"But what if—"

"Seriously, Em. She told us to get out. I'm pretty sure she meant it."

"Whatevs." Emily quirked her lips to the side and stared back down the street toward the Gray's house.

Maddie finished stretching and then hurried inside to shower and get ready for school. But as hard as she tried to forget, she kept seeing Sydney doubled over, clutching her leg.

\*\*\*\*\*\*\*\*\*\*\*\*\*\*\*\*\*\*\*

Maddie slammed her locker shut and glanced at her phone. A text from Dylan illuminated the screen.

What's up? Came by your locker this morning, didn't see you.

Maddie smiled, her heart fluttering in her chest. She only had a couple of minutes to get to her next class, so she sent a message back.

Almost late for school, stopped to help Sydney. She couldn't run.

Maddie hit send and instantly regretted it. Why couldn't she think of something fun or flirty to say? She could've wished him good luck in his first soccer game that night. Talking about his sister was so lame. Shaking her head, she rushed to get to math before the bell rang.

Don't worry about Syd. She'll be fine.

Maddie tucked her phone in the pocket of her hoodie and slid into her seat with only seconds to spare. She wouldn't be able to answer Dylan now. Why wasn't he more concerned about his own twin sister?

After school, Maddie was the last one on to change her clothes and step onto the ice. Sydney was already at the far end of the rink, working on some intricate footwork. She didn't skate like somebody whose leg was killing her. Was this morning all an act? The whole thing was just weird. Maybe she'd worried for nothing. Although the nagging feeling that something wasn't quite right stayed with her, Maddie tried to put Sydney out of her mind and focus on the triple-triple combo. But she couldn't get her timing down and it was a long afternoon, filled with tons of mistakes. By the time practice ended, she couldn't wait to unlace her skates and call it a day.

Alyssa sat on the mats outside the locker room, stretching her leg muscles. Sydney had cleaned off her skates and hurried outside without saying goodbye to anyone.

"What's up with her?" Alyssa asked, her head turned toward the front door as it banged shut behind Sydney.

"Who knows?" Maddie sat on the mat beside her, pointed her toes and leaned her head towards her knees.

"She doesn't talk to anybody but Max."

"Believe me, I've tried. Emily and I found her limping up the hill this morning."

Alyssa's chin dropped. "No way. What happened?"

Maddie sat up and spread her legs wide, leaning forward again and pressing her cheek against the mat. It felt good to stretch. "We walked her home and she tried to blow us off, acted like nothing was wrong."

Alyssa frowned. "Sounds like Tess."

"Tess? Tess Larsen?" Maddie thought of the thin, willowy skater from Magnolia who used to win every junior event she entered. Then one day she just stopped skating.

"She ran all the time, tried to skate with a stress fracture. Then she quit." Alyssa shrugged. "I bet it happens all the time."

Maddie straightened. A stress fracture? Max would never let anybody skate with a stress fracture, although she knew plenty of skaters tried it. It was no secret that anorexia was what really ended Tess's skating career.

"Sydney doesn't look anything like Tess did," Alyssa said.

Maddie nodded. "She looked fine on the ice today."

"No biggie. I still wish she'd talk to us. We're all in this together, you know?"

Maddie finished her stretching and waited for Emily to come out of the locker room. If Sydney didn't care about making friends, then Maddie wasn't going to waste any more time. But an icy ball of worry still lodged in her stomach. Somehow she knew this morning was only the beginning.

\* \* \* \* \* \* \* \* \* \* \* \* \* \* \* \* \* \* \*

Zak rinsed the dinner dishes and Maddie loaded them in the dishwasher. Thank goodness their teachers were going easy on them this first week and they didn't have much homework. She'd hate to miss Dylan's first soccer game. Zak wiped his hands on the towel draped over the oven door handle and tugged his keys from the pocket of his cargo shorts. "Ready?"

Maddie plopped the gel packet of detergent in the dishwasher and closed the door, pressing the "on" button with her index finger. "Yep. Let's go."

Mom glanced up from helping Emily with her reading assignment at the kitchen table. "Come straight home after the game, you two. It's a school night."

"Got it." Maddie followed Zak out to his car, pulling the front door closed behind her. They hopped in Zak's red Camry and pulled out of the driveway.

"Wow," Maddie grimaced and fanned her finger in front of her nose. "What died in here?"

"That's a little something I like to call Perfum de Dick's burgers," Zak said, with an exaggerated flourish of his hand. Then he gunned the engine as Maddie clicked her seatbelt into place.

"It smells like perfume de rotting hockey gear. And take it easy, would you? If Dad sees you driving like a maniac, he'll—"

"He'll what?" Zak looked her way, an easy grin stretched across his face. "Take my keys? Then Mom would have to drive me around. She'd love that."

Maddie frowned. She wished she had a little more of Zak's carefree attitude sometimes.

He cranked up the latest CD from Macklemore on his stereo and had them at the Preston Heights High soccer field in less than ten minutes. The bleachers lining the soccer field were filling up fast. Maddie surveyed the crowd and didn't see anyone she knew by name. Zak waved to a group of his friends sitting on the top row and started climbing. Maddie tagged along behind, hoping to blend in. Her breath hitched in her throat when she realized she'd have to walk right past Mr. and Mrs. Gray.

"Hello, there." Mrs. Gray smiled and waved, gathering her hair at the base of her neck and pulling it over one shoulder.

Maddie swallowed hard. "Hi."

Zak was already fist-bumping and high-fiving each of his buddies. Maddie hoped he would save her a seat. There was no way she was sitting with the Grays. Even if she was there to see Dylan play.

"Sydney couldn't make it tonight. She's a little under the weather." Mr. Gray tipped his chin and crossed his arms over his chest, as though daring Maddie to question him.

"I hope she feels better soon." Maddie hurried to grab a space close to Zak. The metal bleachers were chilly and she jammed her hands into the front pockets of her hoodie.

Dylan started at midfield and dominated the game. West Seattle was no match for Preston Heights and never scored a goal. At halftime, Dylan chugged a bottle of Gatorade then glanced up into the bleachers. His eyes landed on Maddie and he tipped his chin, a smile playing at the edges of his mouth. Her heart hammered in her chest. The second half was almost laughable and Preston Heights won four to zero. Zak was busy flirting with the cheerleaders and dance team, who were all in the stands in their matching outfits and decorated jackets. Every one of them wore a huge bow in their ponytail. Maddie waited patiently for Dylan to make his way toward his parents. She didn't expect him to speak to her, but she could hope. Wiping her sweaty palms on her jeans, she chewed on her lip while he climbed the bleachers.

Mr. Gray was all back slaps and loud praise, while Mrs. Gray squeezed his arm and cooed at him. Maddie wondered what Sydney would think if she were here. She didn't seem like the kind of girl who enjoyed sharing the spotlight, even if it was with her twin brother.

At last, Dylan moved past his parents and stood in front of Maddie. "Hey," he said, sweat slicking his dark hair against his forehead. His cheeks were ruddy, which only made him more adorable.

"Hey," she said. "Good game."

"Thanks. It was a good time. Thanks for coming, I know it's hard to skate and do other stuff, so——"

"No biggie. I do fun stuff all the time." She tried to play it cool but ended up sounding totally lame. *Geez. Get it together.*

"I gotta go. I'll see you tomorrow?" His gaze lingered on hers and all she could do was nod and smile. He joined his parents, throwing a quick wave in Zak's direction. Maddie felt dozens of eyes on her. It was obvious the cheerleaders had observed their whole conversation.

Great.

In the car on the way home, Zak had to get in a few digs. "So, what's up with you and Dylan Gray?"

Maddie glanced out the window as they left the school and headed home, her cheeks warming. She couldn't let Zak know how thrilled she was that Dylan noticed she was there. "Nothing. He just thanked me for coming to his game."

"Well he didn't say thanks to anybody else."

Maddie shrugged. "So?"

"So? I thought every cheerleader in the bleachers was going to come right out of her skin. You better watch out. Those girls don't play nice."

"Whatevs." Maddie tried to pretend she didn't care but her stomach twisted in an anxious knot. That's all she needed. Not only did she have a new arch enemy in Sydney, but now the entire cheer squad hated her, too.

# CHAPTER 12

*Pro: She nails that Salchow like a boss.*
*Con: She needs a miracle to land that triple/triple.*

Maddie slid out of the front seat of Mom's car and shouldered her backpack. "Bye, Mom."

Mom wiggled her perfectly manicured fingertips and reached for her coffee cup in the console. "Bye, sweetheart. Have a great day."

Maddie slammed the car door and turned to climb the steps of the school. She almost tripped over Hilary Davis, Preston Heights High's most popular girl and captain of the cheerleading squad. Hilary narrowed her icy blue eyes and tossed her long, platinum blond air over her shoulder. "Well, well, well. If it isn't Zak's baby sister. I think your mommy took a wrong turn. The middle school's down the road."

Her throat constricting, Maddie attempted to side step Hilary but she only moved closer, blocking her path. "I go to school here."

"Oh?" Hilary leaned in, her gleaming white, perfectly aligned teeth revealed behind a fake smile. "Let me give you some advice. Soccer players aren't into ballerinas."

Maddie wrinkled her nose. "I'm not a ballerina and I don't know what you're talking about."

"I think you do. Everybody saw you drooling all over the new guy last night."

Anger made her blood pump faster. Maddie tipped her chin. "I wasn't drooling."

"I don't think you're getting what I'm trying to say. Back off."

Knees trembling, Maddie cut a wide path around Hilary and made her way inside. She kept her head down, formulating all kinds of snappy comebacks she'd been unable to come up with when Hilary was in her face. Why did she always think of this when it was too late?

Her fingers were still shaking when she got to her locker and tried to twist the combination lock. What was up with that? Dylan probably didn't even know who Hilary was. Yet.

"Hey, what's up?" A familiar voice asked.

Maddie spun around and found Dylan standing behind her, looking amazing in dark washed jeans and a brick red t-shirt. She pasted on a smile. "Hey."

"Is everything okay? You look kinda freaked out." Dylan shoved his hands in his back pockets.

"I'm good. Just thinking about my first class and stuff." Maddie tucked her hair behind her ear. She couldn't tell him what just happened. Totally lame. Sydney already called her a tattle tale once; Maddie didn't need to prove her right.

"Can I walk with you?" Dylan asked.

"To my class?" Maddie's stomach fluttered. Wait till Hilary found about that. She'd flip out.

He shrugged. "Yeah, come on. There's something I want to ask you."

"Okay." Maddie grabbed her book and her notebook and closed her locker. Dylan's shoulder brushed against hers as they walked down the hall. Maddie prayed they wouldn't run into Hilary but half of her wished they would. She licked her lips and tried to pretend as if hot guys walked her to class all the time.

"So I won four tickets to a Katy Perry concert at Key Arena this weekend. Do you want to go?"

Maddie's heart hammered against her chest. She must be hearing things. Did he just ask her out? The world seemed to move in slow motion as she glanced at his face to double check. "Seriously?"

He smiled and she thought her heart would rocket into outer space.

"Seriously." They climbed the stairs to the second level, other students rushing past them, backpacks thumping and conversations echoing off the stairwell. Maddie wished they had ten minutes to get there instead of six. "I haven't asked anybody else yet. Still working on the other two."

Maddie knew her parents would never let her go unless they were super confident that they could trust the other two people in the group. Even then, this was a long shot. But there was no way she was going to tell him no. "I'd love to, thanks for asking."

Dylan stopped at the top of the stairs. "Really?"

She reached the top stair and smiled. "Of course. It sounds amazing."

He pumped his fist in the air. "Sweet. I'll catch you later then."

Maddie clutched her books to her chest and watched him walk away. "See you," she whispered. Maybe she could convince her parents to make an exception to their rules about dating before she was fifteen. She had to find a way.

During English class, she tried to focus on Mrs. Ackerman's lecture but her thoughts kept drifting to Dylan. Did that really just happen? Katie Perry. That concert had been sold out for weeks. She scribbled down the notes from the smart board Mrs. Ackerman projected on the screen at the front of the class. *Focus*. With their trip to Spokane coming up, she couldn't afford to fall behind in her school work the first week of the semester.

After her morning classes were finished, Maddie was on her way to the cafeteria for lunch when her phone chimed again. It was a text from Dylan.

I'll ask Zak and Sydney.

Maddie winced. Not exactly who she had in mind, but now was not the time to complain. Zak hadn't said much about Sydney. Sure, he probably thought she was cute, but going with her to the concert? Didn't sound like his thing.

She pulled the door open and went into the cafeteria, grabbing an orange tray from the stack at the end of the counter. Laughter rang out at a nearby table, while forks scraped against plates and Maddie looked around for a familiar face. Zak and his friends were huddled around a smartphone, but she knew better than to interrupt. He was a great brother, but even he had his limits. Besides, if she wanted him to go on a double-date with her, she'd have to play it cool.

Maddie bypassed the pizza and corn dogs offered as the main entrees and chose a grilled chicken sandwich instead. If she added milk and a cup of fruit, that would be enough lunch to fuel her body for practice this afternoon. Delaney was ahead of her in line, paying for her lunch. Maybe they could sit together. She wasn't with any of the cheerleaders this time. "Hey, Delaney."

Delaney looked over her shoulder and smiled. "Hey, Maddie. How's your eye?"

Maddie touched her fingers to her face. The bruising was easy to conceal with makeup now, but it was still tender to touch. She shrugged. "It's all right."

"Want to grab a table?" Delaney surveyed the cafeteria quickly. "I don't really see anyone I know, except for your brother."

"I don't know any of those guys he's with." Maddie tipped her head toward two vacant seats nearby. "How about right here?"

They set their trays on the table and sat down. Delaney had a salad and a cup of water in front of her.

"Aren't you hungry?" Maddie asked, opening her carton of milk.

"I'm supposed to watch what I eat. The coach wants me to be the flyer." Delaney forked a bite of salad but avoided eye contact.

Maddie stilled. "Delaney, you are tiny. I'm sure the cheerleaders will have no trouble tossing you in the air."

Delaney shrugged. "That's not what coach says."

Maddie took a bite of her sandwich. First Sydney and now Delaney. Didn't grown-ups know they weren't supposed to say stuff like that to girls?

They ate in silence for a few minutes, the controlled chaos of the cafeteria swirling around them. Delaney was petite, tan, and beautiful. She'd obviously worked hard all summer to look hot in her cheerleading uniform. Maddie could relate to the obsession of looking perfect when performing in front of others. But still—

"Do you have Ackerman for English?" Delaney changed the subject. That was a sure sign she didn't want to talk about cheerleading or her weight.

"Yep. She already called me out."

"You? For what? You're always quiet as a mouse in class."

"I was doodling in my notebook. That woman must have radar, because she asked me to talk about The Scarlet Letter." Maddie's cheeks warmed at the memory. She could skate in front of hundreds of people but hated being singled out in class.

"I heard she's really tough, especially on athletes." Delaney sipped her water.

"What did we ever do to her?" Maddie asked.

"Nothing, she just doesn't want anyone to get special treatment."

Maddie filed that away for future reference. She'd be careful not to ask for any special favors unless she really needed it. Usually her teachers were understanding about the demands of the competitive figure skating season. But that was middle school.

"Are you going to the football game at Eastside Catholic?" Delaney asked, her eyes glittering with excitement.

"I think we're in Spokane that weekend. There's a big skating competition."

"Oh." Delaney quirked her lips to one side. "Well, good luck."

"Thanks." Maddie wiped her mouth with her napkin and reached for her container of cantaloupe. A twinge of regret knifed at her. Everyone went to that football game. Nicholas never missed it when he went to Preston Heights, and she'd already heard Zak talking about it. Dylan would probably go, too, if he didn't have a soccer game. She bit her lip. Once she was on the ice in Spokane, football would be the last thing on her mind, but sitting here now with Delaney she felt bad for missing it.

"It's just a game, Mads. Don't look so bummed." Delaney offered a smile.

"Thanks. It's times like these I wish I was a normal teenager." Maddie drained the last of her milk and set the carton on her tray.

"You are a normal teenager. You just happen to like skating, too."

"I always feel a little bit left out when everyone's talking about what they did over the weekend and nobody cares that I landed my first triple Salchow."

Delaney laughed. "Well, when you're on the podium getting your gold medal, we all get to say, 'hey, she goes to my school.'"

Maddie dipped her head. "I don't know about that. The gold medal part, I mean."

"I've seen you skate. I bet you could make it to the Olympics if you work really hard," Delaney said.

A little flutter of excitement rose up within her. She would give anything to make that dream a reality.

The warning bell rang and they all scrambled to clean up their lunches and get to their next class.

"Thanks for sitting with me, Delaney." Maddie smiled and waved to her friend as they parted ways at the double doors.

"You're welcome. See ya, Mads." Delaney disappeared into the throng of students in the hallway.

Maddie climbed the stairs to her next class, still thinking about Dylan's invitation and text message. She could handle missing a football game but she did not want to miss her first official date with the new hot guy. Hilary Davis would be all over him in a second if she found out Maddie had to stay home because her parents said "no." Zak had chemistry near her math class, but she didn't see him in the hallway. She'd have to settle for a quick text. He was always up for a concert, but asking Sydney would take some convincing.

\*\*\*\*\*\*\*\*\*\*\*\*\*\*\*\*\*\*\*

Mom delivered Maddie and Emily to the front door of the rink after school. Thank goodness. So distracted by Dylan's offer, she'd struggled to pay attention at school the rest of the afternoon. She should have asked Mom for permission to go to the concert, but if Mom had said no, Maddie would be crushed. Then she'd be a wreck for practice and Max would be on her case about skating focused. Zak hadn't answered her text, anyway, so she couldn't put her plan for a double-date in place just yet.

"Have a great practice, girls. I'll see you later," Mom said.

"Thanks for the ride, Mom." Emily jumped out of the middle seat and trotted toward the front door of the arena.

"Thanks, Mom." Maddie climbed out and shut the passenger door. Slinging her duffle bag over her shoulder, she went inside. Max and Elise were waiting outside the locker room, writing each skater's name on a scrap of paper and dropping it in a hat. Maddie's heart stuttered. That meant one thing: impromptu program rehearsal. Each girl's name was drawn from the hat and then she had to skate her short program from start to finish in front of the coaches and other skaters.

"Maddie, Emily, nice to see you both." Elise smiled and dropped the papers inside the Seattle Sounders knit hat Max held in his hand.

"Hi," Maddie said, high-fiving Max as she headed for the locker room. Adrenaline was already surging through her. Skating in front of her training partners was the most nerve-wracking sometimes. They knew every twizzle and jump by now, and often had the most critical eye. For all their talk about teamwork, it really was every girl for herself once you stepped on the ice.

Maddie changed into her practice clothes, including black cotton gloves to keep her hands warm. She didn't plan on falling, but it didn't hurt to be prepared for a worst-case scenario. She padded over to the mats to stretch before lacing up her skates. The rest of the girls were still changing and a few were on the ice warming up.

"Maddie, I picked your name first," Max said, walking toward her. "Please warm up as soon as you can."

Maddie swallowed hard and reached for her inhaler. "Okay."

First was great because then she could relax and watch everyone else. But she'd never seen Sydney's short program and that was weighing on her. *It's just practice. Calm down.* Taking a deep breath, she laced up her skates and walked toward the rink. Tugging off her skate guards near the boards, Maddie tossed them on the bench and started her warm-up laps. Mentally, she rehearsed every stroke and technical element in the two minute and thirty second routine. The other girls finished their laps and stepped off the ice, sipping their water and propping their elbows on the boards.

"You ready, Maddie?" Elise called.

Maddie nodded. She skated to center ice and struck a pose. The opening bars of the theme song to Mission Impossible played over the loud speaker and she pushed off with one blade, moving in time to the music. Gaining momentum, her edges carved into the ice as she skated around the rink.

*It will take a miracle to land that triple-triple today.*

*Stop.*

She pushed aside the doubt and kept skating, but it niggled its way back inside her head. At the last minute, she abandoned her opening triple-triple and pulled off a flawless triple Salchow instead. The other girls applauded and she let their enthusiasm buoy her as she tackled the next several elements. Although the Salchow used to send her sprawling, she'd finally nailed it. That in itself was an achievement, but she knew the premier skaters all had opening triple-triple combos and they probably landed them every time.

Maddie ended her program with a near-perfect Biellmann, the advertising on the boards rushing past in a blur of colored graphics as she completed her revolutions. Digging her toe pick into the ice to stop the spin, she flung her arms in the air to signal the end of her program. The music stopped and her teammates clapped and hollered. Maddie smiled and curtsied, trying to mask her disappointment.

"Nicely done." Max motioned for her to join him at the end of the ice, where he'd stood next to Elise, brow furrowed through the whole routine.

"I still say that music is absolutely perfect for you, Maddie." Elise smiled and clapped her on the shoulder.

"Thanks," Maddie said as she filled her lungs with cool air. Pulse still pounding, she skated in a half-circle while her coaches analyzed her performance, her blades carving crescent moons in the ice.

"Your spin at the end was fabulous, everything we want to see in a Biellmann," Max said.

"But I didn't even try the triple-triple," Maddie said.

"That's okay. You'll get it." Elise said.

"If I can't skate it here, what am I going to do in Spokane?" Maddie jammed her hands on her hips and skated another figure eight, trying to stay out of Sydney's way as she warmed up.

"Skating is about more than the elements, Mads. It's about artistry and storytelling, as well," Elise reminded her.

"The only story I'm telling is that I'm too chicken to take a chance," Maddie said.

"Confidence is a big part of your struggle, you're right about that." Max pointed to Sydney. "We'll talk more, but Sydney's up next."

Maddie skated over to the side and reached for the water bottle Alyssa handed her. "Good job, Mads."

"Thanks." Maddie chugged the water and took her place next to Alyssa. Sydney's music wasn't something she'd heard before. It was spunky and alluring at the same time and everyone's eyes were locked on the willowy figure moving gracefully across the ice. But going into her death drop combo, Sydney's blade caught and she crashed to the ice.

The girls all gasped. Sydney was slow to get up, but she finished her routine, anyway. While Maddie knew better than to be happy about her teammate's struggles, she couldn't help but wonder how things would shake out in Spokane.

# CHAPTER 13

*Pro: First double date, first concert with a cute guy ... could this night get any better?*
*Con: No, but it could get worse. Especially if your suspicions are starting to ring true.*

"The answer is still no, Maddie." Mom leaned over the kitchen table and glued another rhinestone on the gauzy bodice of Maddie's costume.

"But it's just a concert, Mom," Maddie protested, stretching the fabric taut so Mom wouldn't snag it with her tweezers.

"It's also you riding alone in a car with a boy you just met."

Maddie gnawed on her lower lip. "What if Zak and Sydney come with us?"

Mom hesitated. "Did you ask Zak how he feels about that?"

"Not yet."

"If Zak drives and there's another girl along, I suppose I might consider it."

Maddie glanced at the clock. Zak had come home from hockey practice a few minutes ago and she could hear him singing in the shower upstairs. It might take some convincing and serious bribery, but there was still time to get him to agree to her plan and text Dylan her answer.

They finished gluing on the rhinestones and Mom hung the red leotard with the flowing skirt up in the mudroom so the glue could dry.

"Do you have tights for this costume?" Mom asked.

Maddie thought about the drawer full of tights in her room. "Probably."

"Go check. We can't get to Spokane and have tights with holes in them." Mom squirted the table with vinegar and water, then wiped it down with a paper towel.

Maddie took the stairs two at a time, new tights really the last thing on her mind. But she knew better than to disobey. Especially if she wanted Mom to give her permission to go out with Dylan. She went into her room and pawed through her collection of clothes for skating. There were at least two pairs of new tights in her drawer that would look great with red. She heard Zak coming out of the bathroom and shoved the drawer closed, running to catch him before he went into his room.

"Hey." She leaned against the doorframe, trying to look casual. "Want to go to the Katy Perry concert tomorrow night?"

Zak arched one eyebrow. "Heck, yeah. Is that what that text was about today?"

"Yep. But you never answered me. Dylan Gray won four tickets. He invited us." Maddie's heart thumped, wondering how she would add the part about Sydney.

Zak narrowed his eyes. "He invited us or he invited you?"

"Both. You, me and Sydney." Maddie smiled. "Do you want to go or not?"

"Wait. Sydney? Like a double date?" Zak raked his hands through his damp hair.

"Nothing serious. Just four friends at a concert."

"Right. Is that what Sydney thinks?"

Maddie shrugged. "I don't know. We haven't talked about it. Dylan just invited me this morning."

"I don't know, Mads. She's cute and all, but I'm not sure I want to get involved. She's got ... issues." Zak wrinkled his nose.

"I'm not asking you to take her to prom. Geez, it's one night." Maddie was growing impatient. This was not going according to plan.

"All right, all right. But it's going to cost you." Zak waggled his eyebrows.

"I'll clean the bathroom for two weeks," Maddie said.

"My bathroom and yours for a month."

"Fine, both bathrooms for a month." Maddie cringed. *Gross.* His bathroom was disgusting, even without Nicholas around. Whatever. She could handle it.

"Garbage, too," Zak added, clearly enjoying himself.

"Fine. Garbage, too. If we need you to drive, what's that going to cost me?" Might as well get it all out in the open. *A date with Dylan. You're getting a date with Dylan, remember?*

"Now the truth comes out." Zak tapped his finger against his chin. "Let me guess: Mom won't let you go unless I drive. This could work out well for me."

"Easy. I'm already doing your chores." Maddie glared at him, annoyed that he'd figured out her angle. He wasn't going to let her live this one down.

"I'm just messing with you. If everybody throws in a few bucks, I'll be golden," Zak said.

"Are you sure?" Maddie didn't want to give him anything else to hold over her head.

"I'm sure. Tell Mom I'll chaperone your date tomorrow." Zak grinned before stepping back and slamming his bedroom door.

"Ha, ha." Maddie thumped his door with her fist and ran back down the stairs.

Mom was at her desk in the kitchen, fingers tapping on the keyboard of her laptop.

"I have new tights and Zak says he'll go with us to the concert," she said breathlessly.

Mom smiled. "You didn't waste any time asking, did you?"

"The concert's tomorrow, Mom. I don't have much time."

Mom stared at her screen for a moment. "I suppose it will be fine.

Just be careful, Mads."

Maddie blew out a breath she didn't realize she'd been holding. "Thanks, Mom."

"You're welcome. Don't make me regret my decision."

"I know. You won't." Maddie dug her phone out of her backpack in the mudroom and texted Dylan the good news.

\*\*\*\*\*\*\*\*\*\*\*\*\*\*\*\*\*\*\*\*

Sydney and Maddie hustled to the Boones's car, Emily trailing along behind them. Practice was grueling today. Max absolutely wore them out. Coupled with the Zumba class she took at the athletic club this morning, her legs felt like Jell-O. But she'd find a way to recover, because nothing would keep them from seeing Katy Perry tonight.

Mrs. Boone smiled when they climbed in the car. "Hi, Sydney. Hi, girls. How was practice?"

"It's over, that's what matters," Maddie said, tugging her seatbelt across her chest.

"That good, huh?" Mom shifted the car into drive and pulled forward to the stop sign.

"Max was all business today," Sydney said, pulling a water bottle from her bag.

"No kidding," Emily said, leaning her head back on the seat. Even the younger girls skated hard today.

"Now you can put it behind you and get ready for the concert," Mom said.

Maddie turned around and smiled at Sydney. "Do you want to come over and we can get ready together?"

Sydney's eyes sparkled. "Really? That would be sweet. What are you wearing?"

Maddie hesitated. She'd agonized over three different outfits last night before bed and still hadn't decided. "I can't decide. Maybe I can show you what I picked out?"

Sydney shrugged. "Sure. I have a shirt my mom designed that would look great on you, especially with your blonde hair. I'll bring it over."

Maddie was certain her surprise was evident by the expression on her face. Was this the same Sydney Gray who barely spoke to her? Skated alone, trained alone, refused almost all conversation on the ice? She found her voice. "Thanks, Sydney."

They dropped Sydney off at her house with the promise to reunite in a few minutes. Maddie had barely climbed out of the shower and pulled on her bathrobe when Mom let her know that Sydney was walking up the driveway. Dang, that girl could hustle. Maddie toweled off her hair while Sydney made her way upstairs.

"That was fast," Maddie said, when Sydney came in to her room, carrying a few outfits on hangers draped over her arm.

"My hair curls better when it isn't freshly washed," Sydney explained, glancing around Maddie's room. "I like your room."

"Thanks." Maddie wondered what sort of a room Sydney had, although she probably hadn't had much time to decorate yet.

"I don't have curtains up or anything yet," Sydney said, as though reading Maddie's thoughts. "We're planning to paint first, but I don't know when that will happen."

"Was it hard to move?" Maddie asked, thinking of Hannah's decision to move to California.

"I guess." Sydney draped the clothes across Maddie's bed. "I was ready for a new start. I don't think Dylan was all that excited."

Maddie winced. She thought Dylan liked it here. At least he acted as though he did. "What do you mean?"

"He's a great soccer player and I don't know if he'll play as much here as he did back ho—in Colorado."

"I hope it works out for him," Maddie said. An awkward silence hung between them for a moment. "Let me dry my hair and then we can figure out the rest, okay?"

"That's cool." Sydney was already mixing and matching different shirts with skinny jeans.

When Maddie finished blowing out her long hair in the bathroom, she found Sydney sitting on the floor in front of Maddie's full-length mirror, patiently curling her own raven locks with the curling iron.

"You can use the bathroom, you know."

Sydney smiled, her eyes meeting Maddie's in the mirror. "That's okay. This works. Look at the outfit I pulled together for you."

Maddie glanced at her bed. Sydney had a white tunic with blue chevron stripes paired with dark washed skinny jeans. Maddie's favorite brown boots were on the floor next to the bed.

"What do you think?" Sydney asked.

"I love it. How did you do that?" Maddie splayed her fingers across her chest. It really was the perfect outfit for her first date and first concert.

"My mom helped me. She designed the shirt but I think it will look better on you," Sydney said, wrapping another section of hair around the wand of the curling iron.

"Wow, I don't know what to say. Thank you."

"Try it on, I want to see how it looks."

\*\*\*\*\*\*\*\*\*\*\*\*\*\*\*\*\*\*\*\*

By the time they finished with their hair and makeup, Dylan was already waiting downstairs with Zak. Sydney went down first and Maddie felt a slow heat climb her neck when she realized all eyes were on them.

Dylan met her gaze and smiled. "Hey."

Maddie swallowed back the butterflies dancing in her stomach. "Hey. Sorry to keep you waiting."

"No worries. You look nice."

"Thanks, so do you." Maddie immediately wanted to snatch the words back. Dylan glanced down at his jeans and dark green t-shirt, a smile on his lips. "I spent hours picking out my outfit."

"Ha, ha." Sydney wacked him on the back. "Guys have it so easy."

"You ready?" Zak grabbed his keys from the kitchen counter.

"Yep." Maddie slipped the strap of her cross-body purse over her head and kissed Mom on the cheek.

Mom gave her shoulders a squeeze. "Have fun, everybody. Be careful."

"We will," they called over their shoulders and sailed out the front door.

Sydney wasted no time snagging shotgun next to Zak, leaving Maddie to sit in back with Dylan. Not that she would complain, but now it really felt like a date. *That's a good thing, right?*

"I say we go with something quick for dinner. Everybody like Five Guys?"

Maddie's mouth practically watered at the thought of burgers and French fries from Five Guys. Fast food was such a rare treat. "I'm in."

"I haven't had a cheeseburger in ages," Sydney said.

"Dylan? You cool with that?" Zak asked, backing out of the driveway.

"Sounds good."

Katy Perry's voice blasted through the speakers when Zak turned on the stereo, and they listened to "Roar" on the way to the nearest Five Guys. Maddie bobbed her head along to the music, too embarrassed to sing out loud in front of Dylan, even though she knew every word.

Zak grabbed the last parking spot in front of the shopping center and they climbed out of the car, Maddie's shoulder brushing against Dylan's as they walked. The smell of French fries wafted toward them and Maddie's stomach growled.

The restaurant was crowded, but they found a table for four by the window. Burgers sizzled on the grill and the guys behind the counter called out orders to each other.

"Ladies, why don't you sit down and we'll get your food?" Zak offered.

"Really? Thanks." Maddie sat down across from Sydney. "I'll have a cheeseburger, no onions, peppers or mushrooms, fries Five Guys style, and a Diet Coke, please."

"Got it," Zak said. "Your order hasn't changed since this place opened, by the way."

Maddie shrugged. "What can I say? I know what I like."

"Sydney? Does Dylan know your order?"

"No way." Dylan held up both hands. "She never orders the same thing twice. Tell him, Syd."

Sydney tucked her hair behind her ear with one hand and studied the menu posted on the sign above the cashier. "You know what I'm craving, like, right now? Bacon. I'll have a bacon cheeseburger, no onions or peppers, fries, and a Diet Coke. Please."

Maddie tried not to let her surprise show this time. She didn't think Sydney even ate meat. Maybe tonight was an exception.

"We'll be back in a few minutes."

Sydney fiddled with the salt and pepper shakers while they waited. "What do you think Spokane will be like? Are the other skaters pretty good?"

Maddie shrugged. "We go every year. There's a couple of girls who are very competitive."

Sydney nodded. "It's so different here. In Colorado, I knew who would be hard to beat and who would probably never skate a clean program. Now I have to start over."

Maddie wasn't sure how to answer that. Sydney obviously didn't like to finish out of the top three. "Every competition is different. That's what Max says. Bring your best effort and that's all you can do."

Sydney frowned. "I still like to know what I'm up against. I guess I'll check them out on line. Everybody has YouTube videos posted now."

"Obvi." Maddie didn't like to spend a lot of time watching the other skaters. She had enough trouble keeping Sydney's performances out of her head. But she wasn't going to admit that now.

Zak and Dylan returned with their food, burgers and fries balanced along with drinks on red trays. "Here you go."

"Let me grab some extra ketchup," Dylan said.

Maddie dug into her cheeseburger, the flavors exploding on her tongue. This was such a rare treat, she intended to savor every bite.

Sydney closed her eyes, chewing her bacon cheeseburger with exaggerated slowness. "OMG, this is sooo good."

Zak shook his head. "You two need to get out more."

"Very funny." Maddie dipped a fry in a pool of ketchup and popped it in her mouth.

"Our soccer coach asked us to cut out all carbonated beverages," Dylan said. "He says we'll play better without it. My coach in Colorado wanted us to drink pop after games. He said it was all part of the refueling process."

"Everything in moderation, dude." Zak bit into the first of two double cheeseburgers. The rest of them could only laugh and shake their heads.

Sydney polished off her burger and pointed at the mini cheeseburger still sitting in front of Dylan. "Are you going to eat that?"

Dylan looked down at his food. "Geez, Syd. Have you eaten today?"

An awkward silence hovered over the table.

"I worked out twice today, thank you very much. If you don't want to share, I'll get my own." Sydney frowned and reached for her purse.

"No, it's cool. You can have it. I probably can't finish it, anyway." Dylan slid his basket toward his twin sister.

Maddie tried to ignore the uneasy feeling that took root in the pit of her stomach. Did Sydney struggle with bulimia? She seemed so happy tonight, her eyes sparkling as she talked to Zak. If she worked out twice today then she'd probably earned every calorie.

Zak checked his phone. "We better get going, the concert starts in forty-five minutes."

They cleaned up the remnants of their meal and headed back out to the car. Traffic crawled into downtown, but Maddie didn't mind, because that meant more time with Dylan. They traded stories about their first concert experiences. His was James Taylor at some place called Red Rocks in Colorado.

"The guy's a legend, I guess, but I was kinda bored," Dylan admitted. "Mom and Dad loved every second, though."

"In my mind I'm going to Carolina ..." Sydney sang.

"How about you, Maddie? First concert?" Dylan's gaze lingered on hers and she felt a shiver of excitement run up her spine.

"Um, One Direction with Emily for her birthday." Maddie smiled. "It was probably better than James Taylor."

"If you like a bunch of screaming little girls losing their minds," Zak grumbled, inching the car forward into a parking garage near Seattle Center.

"I don't get the One Direction obsession," Dylan said.

"Emily loves them. There's a couple of good songs, I guess."

Zak squeezed into a parking space on the upper level of the garage and they all got out, then made their way to the elevator.

Outside, there were people everywhere, streaming toward Key Arena. Zak and Sydney took the lead, merging onto the crowded sidewalk. Dylan reached for Maddie's hand and she smiled up at him, her heart thrumming in her chest as his fingers twined with hers. A hot guy holding her hand and Katy Perry ... could this night get any better?

It took forever to get to their seats, which were on the floor level about twenty rows back from the stage. The opening act, Kacey Musgraves, had already started her first song. She was wearing white shorts and a silver sequined tank top, strumming a guitar while she sang. Maddie had heard the song on the radio a few times, but didn't really know the words. Dylan let go of her hand while she slid into the row, taking the fourth seat. They didn't sit down, because the whole crowd was on their feet, swaying to the folksy rhythm of the song.

Kacey sang a few more songs and then the whole arena went dark. People started cheering and clapping as a silhouetted figure rose up from the center of the stage. A rainbow of colored lights streamed down, putting on an impressive display before the spotlight turned and illuminated Katy Perry. The whole place went nuts. Katy Perry sang song after song and the crowd stayed on their feet, pounding their fists in the air in time to the music. Maddie longed for a slow ballad so she could sit and soak it all in. Dylan slipped his arm around her shoulders and she soon forgot how tired her legs were.

The fireworks that exploded on stage when Katy actually sang "Firework" were unlike anything Maddie had ever seen. Her mouth dropped open as the show only got better with each passing minute. She leaned in front of Dylan and yelled to Zak, "This is amazing!"

Kacey Musgraves came back onstage and they sang a duet, something Maddie had never heard before. The grand finale was a duet of "Roar," which everyone loved. When the lights went up and everyone filed toward the exits, Maddie was a little disappointed that it was over so quickly.

On the walk back to the car, Dylan reached for her hand again. "Well? Did you like it?"

"It was epic," Maddie said, squeezing his hand. "Thanks for inviting me."

"Yeah, dude. Thanks." Zak said over his shoulder. "Those seats were pretty sweet, too."

Dylan shrugged. "Glad you liked it. Totally random call to the radio station. I never thought I'd win."

"I like that Kacey girl," Sydney said. "She's way different from most country artists."

"Mom would freak if she heard those lyrics," Zak said.

Maddie couldn't agree more and made a mental note to change the station the next time one of Kacey's songs came on.

Sydney yawned loudly. "I'm going to sleep all the way to Spokane tomorrow."

"Me, too," Maddie said, stifling a yawn of her own. That early morning workout at the club was catching up with her.

By the time they got back to Zak's car, Maddie was almost asleep on her feet. She sank into the back seat and tipped her head back.

"Here," Dylan patted his shoulder. "You're exhausted. Take a nap. I'll wake you up when we get to your house."

"Thanks." Maddie leaned her head against his shoulder. She meant to tell him again how much fun she'd had, but the words never made it past her lips.

The next thing she knew, the car had stopped.

"Maddie?" Dylan whispered. "We're home."

He planted a soft kiss on her forehead. Maddie's eyes popped open. Did he really just kiss her forehead? She sat up straight, squinting into the darkness. They were in the Gray's driveway. "Wow, I can't believe I fell asleep so fast. How lame is that?"

"Don't worry about it. Thanks for coming tonight. I had a great time."

"Thanks. Me, too." Maddie squeezed his hand and he climbed out of the car.

"Thanks, guys," Sydney said. "See you tomorrow, Maddie."

"Later," Zak said. Maddie could only wave, then touched her fingers to her forehead. Tonight was absolutely perfect. She watched Sydney walk up the steps to her front door. Well, almost perfect. She was convinced Sydney had some kind of an eating disorder. But she pushed that thought out of her mind. No sense ruining an awesome first date worrying about that.

# CHAPTER 14

*Pro: Super pumped for a big competition in Spokane against some talented skaters.*
*Con: Enthusiasm wanes when Sydney seems to be getting worse.*

It was still dark outside when Maddie's alarm on her phone started ringing. She pulled the covers up over her head and snuggled back under the covers. Katy Perry's voice, Dylan's smile, and his arm around her carried her back to dreamland. She didn't want to wake up yet. That would mean the end of her dreams and the cold reality of getting up and driving to Spokane.

The door opened and Maddie heard muffled footsteps on the carpet. "Maddie, it's time to wake up," Mom said.

Maddie groaned and pulled the covers tighter against her chin.

If you want to shower, you'd better get moving. We're leaving in forty-five minutes."

Maddie flung back the covers and kicked her feet over the side of the bed. Yes, a shower before a six-hour car ride would be nice. She grabbed some clean clothes and padded into the bathroom. The mirror was still foggy; Emily must have just finished.

When she came downstairs, Mom was serving bowls of oatmeal from the crock pot. Maddie poured some orange juice and sat down at the table across from Dad.

"Well?" Dad looked up from the newspaper, his eyes twinkling with amusement. "How was the concert?"

Maddie took a long sip of her juice then set the glass down. "It was fun."

"Just fun?" Mom set the bowl of oatmeal in front of Maddie and stepped back. "Not epic? Unbelievable? The best night of your life?"

Maddie rubbed her eyes. "I'm not awake yet. It was epic."

"Did Sydney and Dylan have a good time?" Dad asked.

Maddie shrugged. "I think so."

"I can see I'm going to have to quiz Zak if I want any juicy details." Dad took a sip of his coffee.

"Yep." Maddie loaded her spoon with oatmeal and took a bite. It wasn't her favorite, but it would keep her from eating a bunch of junk food on the long car ride.

Emily came downstairs, dragging an overstuffed duffle bag behind her. She had braided her hair and was wearing a pink velour warm-up suit. Dropping her stuff by the door, she came to the table and sat down.

"Is Alyssa riding with us?" Maddie asked.

"Yes, which is why I need you to hurry. It would be nice if we could load the car when they get here and then be on our way." Mom packed bottled water into a cooler, giving both Maddie and Emily meaningful looks.

"All right, all right." Maddie knew better than to mess with Mom's itinerary for the weekend. She probably had it plotted down to the minute. Rinsing her bowl and her glass, she slid them both in the dishwasher and ran back upstairs to grab her stuff.

A text message was waiting on her phone.

I had fun last night. Good luck this weekend.

Maddie smiled. Dylan. She clutched her phone to her chest. It was going to be hard to concentrate on skating now, but she had to find a way to put Dylan out of her mind, at least for this weekend. She sent a quick message back and sighed.

"Alyssa and Taylor are here with Taylor's mom." Emily leaned against the doorframe. "Who are you texting at six-thirty in the morning?"

"No one." Maddie jumped up and stuffed her phone in her purse.

"I bet it was Dylan." Emily dashed back down the stairs before Maddie could argue.

Carrying her bags downstairs, Maddie found Alyssa and Taylor waiting by the front door, hands jammed in the front pockets of their hoodies. "Good morning."

"Hey," the girls said.

"We can throw your stuff in the back of the car. Your mom has everything just about packed," Taylor said.

"I can carry something." Alyssa held out her hand and Maddie passed her a pillow.

Out in the driveway, Sydney and her mom stood off to the side, watching as Mrs. Boone and Mrs. Quirk packed two SUVs with pillows, duffle bags and figure-skating gear. Just when Maddie didn't think they could fit anything else in, Mrs. Quirk managed to squeeze two more bags in the back of her suburban.

"Okay, ladies." Mrs. Quirk slammed the hatch. "Let's get this show on the road."

Sydney and her mom climbed in the Boones's car, while Alyssa quietly climbed in the back seat of Taylor's car. Maddie couldn't help but notice something seemed a little "off" with Alyssa. Normally a perky morning person, she'd barely smiled when Maddie came downstairs. She'd have to ask her what was up later.

After a pit stop at Starbucks, they were finally on their way. Maddie sipped her skinny vanilla latte from the middle seat, listening as Emily campaigned for a movie in the car's DVD system. Mom finally gave in, probably so she could talk to Sydney's mom in peace. Sydney, meanwhile, had claimed the back seat and shoved her pillow up against the window. She was devouring a cranberry orange scone, a large coffee in the cup holder next to her. She'd also shoved her ear buds in her ears already, a definite sign she wanted to be left alone. So much for bonding on the long ride. Shifting in her seat, she watched Tangled with Emily for at least the fifth time.

By the time the credits rolled, they were exiting the freeway in Moses Lake for a bathroom stop. Inside the convenience store, Maddie wandered along the aisles, waiting for Sydney to come out of the bathroom. She was taking forever. One by one, the other girls bought a bottle of water or a magazine and headed back to the car, but still no Sydney.

Maddie went into the bathroom and leaned down. She could see someone kneeling in front of the toilet in the last stall. Her heart stuttered. Was Sydney sick? The stomach flu was the last thing they needed, especially during a competition.

"Sydney?" Maddie whispered.

The only response was the unmistakable sound of someone vomiting.

*Ewww.* Maddie swallowed hard and knocked on the closed door of the stall.

"Sydney? Are you okay?"

Silence. Then Maddie heard her sniffling and tugging paper off the roll.

"Sydney, it's me, Maddie. Are you sick?"

"Go away. I'll be out in a minute."

"Do you want me to get your mom? I could—"

"No." Sydney flushed the toilet and yanked open the door, her eyes red. "I'm not a baby. I can throw up all by myself. Pretty impressive, right?"

Maddie shrunk back against the bathroom wall. "I was just trying to help."

"Yeah?" Sydney turned around at the sink, water spraying as the sensors came on and she washed her hands. "I don't need your help."

"If you have the stomach flu, we should tell someone. Otherwise everyone could get it."

Sydney laughed, a hollow, bitter sound unlike anything Maddie had heard before. "Oh, Maddie. You're so naïve. I don't have the stomach flu. And if you tell anyone about what you just saw, I'll make sure Dylan never speaks to you again."

Maddie's breath hitched. *What was that supposed to mean?*

Sydney ripped some paper towels from the dispenser and left the bathroom without a backward glance.

Maddie stared after her. How could she possibly turn Dylan against her that fast? What would she say? They hardly knew each other. And Maddie wasn't naïve. She knew plenty of girls who struggled with bulimia. She'd never encountered it firsthand. Her mind raced. Max and Elise were already in Spokane. Should she call and let them know what she witnessed? *No.* Something about Sydney's expression and tone of voice told her she wasn't messing around.

Maddie made her way back to the car, avoiding eye contact with Sydney when she sat in her seat. Of course, Sydney made it easy since she'd already closed her eyes and tucked her ear buds back in her ears. *Whatever.*

Emily finished watching Tangled and started The Cutting Edge. Even though it was one of her favorites, Maddie couldn't concentrate. She kept thinking about Sydney. Did Dylan know what was going on? Didn't twins know everything about each other? Maybe that was just in books and movies. She listened to Mrs. Gray and Mom chatting away in the front seat. They were talking about landscaping and the hospital's fall fundraisers. *Bor-ing.*

Maddie drew in a deep breath and let it out slowly. If she could only go back in time and erase what she'd witnessed in the bathroom. Because she certainly wasn't going to forget it, despite Sydney's warnings. She had to find a way to get Sydney some help without it costing her a relationship with Dylan.

\*\*\*\*\*\*\*\*\*\*\*\*\*\*\*\*\*\*\*

Mom handed Maddie a bottle of water and kissed her cheek. "Good luck, sweetie. I'll be cheering for you."

Maddie took the water and smiled. "Thanks, Mom."

Alyssa sat next to her at the Spokane Arena, her leg bouncing up and down so hard she was rocking their bench. They'd finished their warm up and were waiting for the first competitor to take the ice.

Mom turned to walk away but then turned back. "Alyssa, are you all right, hon?"

Alyssa bit her lip, eyes welling with tears. *Oh no.* Maddie put her arm around her friend's shoulders.

"I think this is my last competition," Alyssa said, pressing her hands to her cheeks.

"Why?" Maddie asked, glancing at her Mom for help.

"It's so expensive and my parents are having a hard time right now. My sister needs so much extra stuff and there's just never enough—"

"Oh, sweetheart, it's okay." Mom sat down on the other side of Alyssa and handed her a tissue. "That's a lot for you to be carrying around when you're supposed to be competing tonight."

"I can't help it." Alyssa dabbed at her cheeks. "I told them I would quit skating if they needed me to, but I didn't really mean it."

Maddie wrinkled her nose. That would suck. Alyssa had five brothers and sisters, but Camden was on the autism spectrum and needed a lot of therapy. But it didn't seem fair that Alyssa should give up skating.

"You still get to skate this weekend, Lys. I think you should have fun and try to do your best. What if you win?" Maddie nudged her friend with her shoulder, hoping to see a smile. All she got were more tears.

"Maddie's right. Have fun and do your best. Don't worry about the future. I know your parents are very proud of you," Mom said.

Alyssa nodded. "Okay, I'll try."

"Good evening, ladies and gentlemen." The announcer's voice boomed over the loudspeaker. "Welcome to the Inland Empire Skate Fest here in beautiful Spokane, Washington."

Applause rang out through the arena and Maddie felt the butterflies begin their usual swirl through her stomach. Alyssa dried the last of her tears and clapped, too, the glitter in her short hair catching some of the overhead light and sparkling.

"Taking the ice tonight, representing the Emerald City Skate Club in Seattle, please welcome Taylor Quirk," the announcer bellowed.

Alyssa and Maddie whooped and cheered as their friend skated around the rink, then posed at center ice. The music started and Taylor dazzled them all with her spunky personality and athletic prowess. Alyssa clutched Maddie's arm with her fingers and they both held their breath whenever Taylor landed a big jump or nailed some intricate footwork. At the end, they clapped and cheered some more as Taylor skated toward them, beaming.

"Great job, Taylor," Maddie said, high-fiving her friend.

"Thanks," Taylor said, chest heaving as she slipped on her skate guards. Max and Elise moved in, offering praise and encouragement. Elise went off with Taylor to the kiss and cry to await the judges' scores, while Max eyed Taylor and Alyssa.

"Should you be sitting down right now? C'mon. On your feet, stay loose." He wiggled his fingers for them to stand up.

Maddie obeyed, shaking out her arms and legs as she stood. She leaned one way and then the other, pretending to stretch, but her eyes were glued to the ice where Sydney was about to skate. Something told her she shouldn't watch, but Maddie couldn't resist. Surely someone with a serious illness who couldn't finish her run wouldn't skate well, would she?

Oh, but she could. Every jump was explosive, her footwork amazing and Sydney really knew how to play to the crowd, as well as the judges. With each element that Sydney nailed, Maddie's doubts about her own short program grew. When the music stopped, Sydney thrust both fists in the air and everyone in the arena could probably read her lips as she yelled, "Yes!"

It was a clean program; she had every right to be proud of herself. Maddie pressed her lips into a thin line and looked away. Max was watching her, brow furrowed.

"Does that worry you?"

Maddie gulped. "Does what worry me?"

"Sydney. Skating like that. Does it worry you?" Max stood next to her, arms folded across his chest.

"I-I don't know. Yeah. Sort of." She looked down at her skates. *You are so lame. Why didn't you play it off?*

"Let me tell you something, Maddie. You are more talented than most of the girls here tonight. You have raw, athletic ability that most people only dream of."

Maddie looked up and smiled, the burden of her jealous emotions easing slightly.

"Now go out there and use it." Max placed both hands on her shoulders and ducked down, staring straight into her eyes. "Do you hear me?"

Maddie nodded. "Yes."

"Good. Now get out there and have fun." Max dropped his hands to his sides and stepped out of her way.

Maddie walked to the side of the rink, watching as the little girls in their precious costumes—the sweepers—collected the flowers and stuffed animals tossed on the ice for Sydney.

She pulled off her skate guards and left them on the boards. Taking a quick lap around the ice, she drew in a deep breath and let it out, trying to slow her racing pulse. This was crazy. It was one competition, less than three minutes of toe loops, layback spins and jump combos she could probably do in her sleep right now. But still the nerves were getting the best of her.

*Stop. Just stop. Focus.*

One more lap, then the announcer gave her introduction. She smiled for the judges and took her place near the center of the rink. She heard the music start and her body responded on cue. Her double Axel was awesome, complete with a flawless landing. Maddie smiled and the crowd cheered. A little transition footwork and then it was time for her spread Eagle. *Hips rotated out. Good. Don't lose your balance ... yes.* She sensed from the crowd's reaction that it was stunning. Another smile for the judges as she sailed by, using every part of the ice the way she was supposed to. Her confidence soared but her legs already felt tired. Pushing herself, she skated on one leg and moved right into her sit spin. *Almost done.* Then she envisioned Sydney skating so well, and under-rotated her spin. Losing momentum, she touched the ice with her hand to get back up. A major deduction. With a flourish, she posed for the last beat of the music and tried to smile.

The applause was generous but she knew it wasn't her best effort. With a heavy heart, Maddie glided toward Max and Elise.

"Good job, Maddie," Elise handed her skate guards and water over the boards.

"I totally messed up," Maddie said, gasping for air. "My spin … it was terrible."

"Shhh, you did fine." Elise tucked her hand into the crook of Maddie's elbow and walked with her to the kiss and cry.

Maddie sank onto the folding chair and Elise took her place next to her. Maddie's heart pounded in her chest, less from exertion and more from the anticipation of the judges' scores. The numbers went up on the board and Maddie squeezed her water bottle so tight, the plastic crinkled in protest.

As predicted, the numbers were lower than she'd hoped for. There was definitely a deduction for her botched sit spin. Maddie tried to keep a brave face but she knew those scores spelled trouble.

Elise hugged her. "I'm proud of you. You should be proud, too. That was a great effort."

Maddie refused to cry in front of everyone. She bit the inside of her cheek hard and shrugged. "It was okay. I can do better."

"That's what we like to hear." Elise patted her leg and stood up to go watch the rest of the competitors.

Maddie took off her skates and pulled on her warm ups, sliding her feet into her running shoes. She took her time cleaning off her skates and tucking them inside her bag for tomorrow's free skate. All she wanted to do now was eat some dinner and crash at the hotel. But there were plenty of skaters left to watch, including Alyssa. With a heavy sigh, Maddie made her way back to the rink and sat down with Taylor to watch the remaining short programs.

Sydney sat a few seats away with her mother. Mrs. Gray wrapped a bag of ice around Sydney's lower leg with an Ace bandage. Maddie tried not to stare but she couldn't help but wonder what was really going on. So her mom knew about her leg but not about the upchucking? So weird. Maddie turned back to the ice, resisting the temptation to tell Taylor the whole story. But Sydney's words about Dylan replayed in her head and she kept silent.

\*\*\*\*\*\*\*\*\*\*\*\*\*\*\*\*\*\*\*\*

The next day, Maddie and the other girls tried to pass the time with a walk through Riverfront Park in downtown Spokane. It was a beautiful late summer day and they posed for lots of pictures. Sydney even managed to join in the fun and smile for the camera phones. For a little while, Maddie almost forgot they were there to skate.

But by the time they got to the rink, her nerves were starting to get the best of her. She usually skated last or next to last because she was often in first after the short program. But last night's mistake had cost her that coveted first place position going into the free skate. That spot belonged to Sydney and Maddie had to skate in the middle of the flight this time.

She couldn't even watch the other performances. Staying in the athlete's lounge—just a curtained off area in the back of the arena—but at least she didn't have to see the other skaters or their final scores. When it was almost her turn, Elise came and let her know. Maddie shed her warm ups and moved toward the rink, heart beating double time the closer she got to the ice.

After a quick warm-up lap, she stopped near the middle of the rink and waited for the music to start. The opening bars of "Phantom of the Opera" streamed through the loudspeaker and Maddie pushed off with her skates, stroking hard to gain enough momentum for her opening triple-triple combo. At the last second, her confidence waivered and she switched to a double Axel, double Toe loop combination, but at least it was flawless. She was so proud of herself, the rest of the program felt like a breeze. Gliding over the ice, Maddie smiled at the judges and pushed through the fatigue. The last forty-five seconds were always the hardest, when her legs were protesting and her chest felt tight. But she kept skating, incorporating every required element and the full eight rotations for her layback spin. By the end of the program, adrenaline surged through her extremities as she jammed her toe pick into the ice and spread her arms wide in a final flourish. *Finally*. A clean long program she could be proud of.

Max and Elise waited for her at the edge of the rink, all smiles and hugs.

"We're so proud of you, Maddie," Elise said. "That was beautiful."

Maddie nodded, too worn out to even speak. She managed a smile and reached for her water bottle, gulping down several sips. In the kiss and cry, Maddie tried to control her breathing while they waited for the judges' scores.

"That layback spin at the end was perfection," Max said, patting her back.

Maddie's heart soared. His words of affirmation meant so much to her because he doled them out sparingly.

The scores went up and the crowd applauded. Her efforts had landed her in second place, but there were two skaters remaining, including Sydney. Maddie hugged her coaches and then took her time putting on her warm ups and cleaning up her skates. The gasp of the crowd told her the girl from Spokane, slated as the hometown favorite, had fallen already. A few minutes later, Maddie watched her leave the ice in tears. Maddie's heart ached for her. She'd been there. It was so hard not to crack under pressure.

Maddie didn't want to watch Sydney skate, but she forced herself to sit in the first row with everyone else from Emerald City and support her teammate. The entire program was breathtaking. Maddie had to admit, Sydney took the competition to a whole another level. Before Sydney finished and the scores went up, Maddie already knew Sydney had won. Although she smiled and offered Sydney congratulations, even shaking her hand on the podium later, she was secretly a little frustrated that Sydney had done so well. If she skated like that injured, she would certainly blow them all away when she was healthy. But Maddie knew she couldn't dwell on that. It had been a great weekend and she let her confidence in her long program carry her forward. Regionals were coming and she intended to be fully prepared.

# CHAPTER 15

*Pro: Skating competitions make all the early morning practices worth it.*
*Con: If skating's so fun, where did all these nerves come from?*

The next week went by in a blur. After spending the weekend in Spokane, Maddie wanted nothing more than a break from the demands of skating and school. She'd tried to study on the long ride home in the car, but it was too easy to watch a movie or listen to music. Mom had reminded her several times that she had a paper due and a math test. Maddie nodded in agreement, but procrastinated a little longer.

She came home from school one afternoon just as Dad was pulling into the driveway with Nicholas in the passenger seat. He must have flown home for his fall break from Stanford. Maddie squealed and ran to his side of the car, waiting impatiently for him to climb out.

"Hey, Mads." Nicholas smiled when he got out, wrapping her in a hug. "How's it going?"

"Good," Maddie said, her cheek against his chest. She patted his back and pulled away to really look at him. His brown hair was a little shaggier than when he'd left and he had the whole dark-rimmed glasses, hipster thing going on. "How's Stanford?"

He shrugged. "It's cool. I like it." He reached back in the car and pulled his backpack out. Dad had already popped the trunk and set Nicholas's suitcase on the driveway.

"Maddie, do you need to get to practice?"

Maddie nodded. "Mom said you could take me. Emily's sick."

Dad paused and glanced at his watch. "Grab your stuff and jump in, then."

Maddie ran back inside for her skates and the rest of her practice gear. Emily was on the couch, watching TV and clutching a bottle of Gatorade. The stomach bug had taken her down hard this week. Maddie was keeping her fingers crossed that she wouldn't catch it. That was the last thing she needed.

On the way to the rink, Dad listened to NPR, brow furrowed as he drove.

"Dad?" Maddie asked. "Can I ask you something?" She rarely had time alone with him, between his demanding schedule at the children's hospital and her skating. But she knew he'd respond better to the plan she was formulating.

"Sure, sweetheart. What is it?" Dad turned down the radio and glanced her way.

Maddie took a deep breath. "I know you and Mom don't want me seeing Dylan like we're boyfriend and girlfriend, but here's the thing: we *never* see each other. I wanted to invite him over to hang out one night this week, if that's cool with you guys." She huffed out a breath, her heart racing. There. She'd asked.

"Your mom and I have talked to you girls a lot about balancing skating and your school work. Now Nicholas is home for a long weekend, I'm not sure it's fair to him if Dylan's hanging around."

Maddie groaned inwardly. That wasn't the answer she expected. Dad was supposed to be on her side. "But Nicholas wouldn't care if I had a friend over. Why is Dylan any different?"

"You know as well as I do that having a boy over is much different than if Taylor or Alyssa came over," Dad said.

Maddie stared out the window. She loved her brother Nicholas and it would be fun to have him home, even if it was only for a few days. But she'd hardly seen Dylan since the Katy Perry concert. He wasn't answering her texts very often and he certainly hadn't called her. She couldn't help wondering if his twin sister had anything to do with this.

*That's crazy.* Maddie hadn't mentioned a word to anyone about what she saw in the bathroom on the way to Spokane. After Sydney won the skate fest, Maddie was afraid to bring it up. She'd end up looking like the jealous teammate who got second place.

"What's going on in that pretty little head of yours?"

Maddie gnawed on her thumbnail. "I just really like Dylan and want to have him over, that's all."

"I'll talk to your mom tonight, but I can almost guarantee she'll say the same thing. Family time is important and sometimes that means we say no to other activities. Including Dylan."

Dad stopped the car in front of the ice rink and Maddie got out of the car.

"Have a great practice, sweetie." Dad winked before she slammed the door shut.

"Whatevs," she whispered as he drove away, her stomach twisting in a knot. She'd have to find some other way to see Dylan.

\*\*\*\*\*\*\*\*\*\*\*\*\*\*\*\*\*\*

Exhausted from her early-morning workout the next day, Maddie dragged herself up the stairs of Preston Heights High. Her phone chimed in her backpack but she waited until she got to her locker to check it. A message from Dylan waited for her. He wanted to meet for lunch. Her heart skipped a beat. After a quick exchange of text messages before the bell rang, they agreed to meet in the cafeteria. A million other places would be so much more fun, but she couldn't go off campus as a freshman. Her parents would totally flip if she went out to lunch with Dylan alone, anyway.

The morning dragged by. Maddie did her best to focus in her classes, but every time she glanced at the clock, it seemed the hands had barely moved. At last, it was lunch and she threw her books in her locker and practically ran to the cafeteria.

Nothing looked remotely appealing so she settled on chicken noodle soup and a small salad, with fruit for dessert. Her stomach was doing back flips anyway at the sight of Dylan sitting alone with his food at the far end of a nearby table. She doubted she'd be able to eat until she heard what he had to say.

"Hey," he said, offering a shy smile as she sat down across from him.

"What's up?" She tried to play it cool, but her heart was beating so loud, he could probably hear it.

"I hadn't seen you in a while. Seems like you're always skating or I'm playing soccer."

She frowned, looking down as she stirred her soup. "I'm sorry, Dylan. I wish I had more time. Until my competitions are over, it's kind of eat, sleep, go to school and skate."

"Sydney said you'd met somebody else, anyway." Dylan avoided eye contact as he dropped this juicy tidbit of news.

Maddie clenched her jaw. "I'm sorry, what?"

Dylan looked up, his lips twisting into a frown. "She said that's all you talked about on the ride to Spokane was this hot guy in your English class."

Maddie's face grew hot as the blood rushed to her head. That girl had some nerve. "Look, I know she's your twin, but do you believe everything she tells you?"

He shrugged. "Yeah. I have no reason not to."

"I barely spoke to Sydney last weekend and if there's a hot guy in my English class, I haven't noticed."

Dylan pushed a slice of pizza around his plate. "So does that mean you'd go to the movies with me this weekend?"

Maddie felt a smile tug at the corners of her mouth. "I have to skate in Tacoma, but I'm free on Sunday."

"Sweet. I'll give you a call. And I'll tell Sydney to mind her own business." Dylan squeezed her hand. "I've got to meet Mr. Wallace before class to talk about my midterm grade. Catch you later."

"Bye," Maddie said, the warmth of his fingers on hers staying with her long after he disappeared through the double doors of the cafeteria. She finished her lunch and tried not to think about all the nasty things she wanted to say to Sydney right now. She should've known that girl was up to something.

*********************

Just minutes after they arrived at the Tacoma Dome the free skate on Friday night, Maddie watched Sydney limping toward the locker room. Served her right. She'd ignored Sydney all week at practice, too angry to trust herself to speak. There was no reason for Sydney to mess up Maddie's chances with Dylan, especially since Maddie had kept her end of the deal. "Hey, Maddie." A few of the girls from the Magnolia skate club walked by, waving as they passed.

Maddie smiled and waved back. Having the competition in Tacoma meant they were much closer to home and could even sleep in their own beds between the short and long programs. It also meant they knew all of the competitors very well and coaches would spend a lot of time analyzing and re-analyzing various skaters and their programs.

Inside the locker room, Maddie sat down and unzipped her bag. Someone was crying in the bathroom stall and Maddie got up and tiptoed up to the door to listen. She could see Alyssa standing inside, her face in her hands.

"Lys? It's me, Maddie. What's wrong?" Maddie tapped on the door with her fingertips.

"Please leave me alone," Alyssa said.

"But you're crying. I want to help."

Alyssa blew her nose and then unlocked the door. Her eyes were red and puffy, her nose still running. She yanked more paper from the roll and swiped at the moisture on her face. "What's going on?" Maddie asked again.

"I'm so sick of my parents spending all of their time and money on Camden and ignoring the rest of us. It wouldn't kill them to come and watch me skate. We don't live that far away. But no, gas is too expensive, Camden had a rough day …" Alyssa pressed her lips into a thin line and shook her head.

Maddie's heart ached for her friend. "I'm really sorry."

"It's not your fault. I just wish they acted as if they cared. What I do matters, too, you know?"

Maddie nodded. "You're a great skater. Max and Elise are super proud of you."

Alyssa blew out a ragged breath. "Thanks."

"Come on, it's almost our turn to warm up." She tugged at Alyssa's sleeve and together they put on their skates and stepped onto the ice.

The jumbotron, combined with the rows upon rows of seats that were gradually filling up, turned Maddie into a bundle of nerves. Her stomach clenched and her chest felt tight. She skated by Max and Elise for another sip of water and a puff on her inhaler. She even did her best to avoid watching Sydney practice her jumps at the other end of the rink. This wasn't even regionals and she was already a mess.

Mom had told her that she'd read online that some of the best skaters in the world blocked everything else out in the minutes before competition. Maddie had seen those skaters on TV, sitting alone or running through their routine on dry land before they even put their skates on. Maybe she should try that instead of watching everyone else skate or surfing through Instagram on her phone.

They were called off the ice so the competition could begin. Maddie popped her ear buds in as soon as she got off the ice and listened to some of her favorite Carrie Underwood songs while she waited her turn. She couldn't sit still, so she sat on the mats and kept stretching. At least she couldn't hear the noise from the crowd or see what the other skaters were doing. But her new plan didn't do anything to ease her anxiety. She took another sip of water, but the tightness in her chest didn't subside. Great. Add the threat of an asthma attack to her list of worries.

Alyssa came off the ice all smiles, the tears from the locker room already forgotten. Her scores were awesome and Maddie turned off her music to pull Alyssa into a hug.

"Congratulations, I knew you could do it," Maddie said.

"Thank you." Alyssa clapped her hands softly, her excitement almost palpable. "I can't wait to watch you skate."

Maddie winced. "Thanks. I'm so nervous tonight. I don't know why."

Alyssa arched one eyebrow. "Do you need a pep talk?"

"That's my job." Max stood at Maddie's elbow, eyes dancing. He loved the intensity and adrenaline rush of competition.

Not even the news that Sydney had fallen during her short program could cheer Maddie up.

"What's the matter? You look as though you saw a ghost." Max gripped her elbow, walking beside her as she headed for the rink.

"I'm really nervous tonight. I don't know why."

"Listen. Your jumps are powerful, your spins like no other girl out here tonight. You can do this. Take it one second at a time," Max said.

Maddie reached the edge of the ice and removed her skate guards. The place was packed. Little girls were clapping and cheering; cameras flashed around the arena. Her picture was even on the jumbotron as she stopped in front of Elise.

"So proud of you, girl. Knock 'em dead." Elise smiled and took her skate guards from her. Maddie wanted to grab them back and go hide in the locker room. As the announcer said her voice over the loudspeaker and she stepped onto the ice, she wondered if she'd be the first to get sick before the music even started.

*Get a grip.*

The girl who skated last tonight was taking up every allotted minute of her warm up so Maddie used that to her advantage and took an extra warm up lap of her own. Breathe. Just breathe. You've done this a bazillion times.

The announcer gave the official introduction and she mustered her brightest smile as she took her place and waited. From the first strokes of her skates as she glided backward in a wide curve, her anxiety melted away. When she planted her toe pick in the ice and launched into the air, she got more height on her triple Lutz than she ever had before. Not even a wobble when she landed, either. She could tell by the applause of the crowd at the end and her coaches' expressions that she'd nailed it. In the kiss and cry, the sweepers filled her arms with lots of thoughtful tossies—roses, stuffed animals, and more flowers that she couldn't even name. The scores went up and Max pumped the air with his fist. "Yes!"

Elise kissed the top of her head.

Maddie was in first after the short program, her strongest finish ever. Maybe those nerves were worth it.

*******************

In the long program the next night, Sydney looked awful and barely finished. She limped off the rink in tears as soon as the music ended, complaining about her leg. Mr. and Mrs. Gray swooped in and bookended her on either side, hovering and asking a million questions. The crowd's uncertainty was evident by their murmurs and subdued applause.

Maddie turned in her seat to exchange worried glances with Dylan, several rows back. He shrugged, his brow furrowed. Maddie turned back around before Max or Elise caught her. They would not be happy if they knew she even acknowledged Dylan's presence. They were probably right; she needed to stay focused. But she also had the luxury of skating last tonight and she wanted to watch Taylor and Alyssa skate, too. Unfortunately, that also meant watching a skater from Magnolia perform a very clean program that earned incredible marks.

Maddie winced and hustled to the edge of the rink for her warm up. Although she wasn't nearly as anxious as the night before, something felt a little off right from the first stroke of her skates. Nothing disastrous, but she felt guarded, like every element was a battle. Her chest burned and her legs refused to cooperate. She skated harder and pushed her way through every element—it was a battle of wills between her brain and her body to make it through the last minute. At the end, she knew in her heart it wasn't her best effort.

Max and Elise acknowledged the good things she did while they waited in the kiss and cry for her scores. But Maddie knew they were confused and disappointed. Probably worried about Sydney, too. When the final numbers went up, the girl from Magnolia sat in first. Maddie finished second. Again. Taylor surprised everyone with a third-place finish and Alyssa trailed by only a few points to claim fourth.

Maddie unlaced her skates and pulled them off, cleaning the blades before storing them back in her bag. It wasn't at all how she expected things to turn out. Second place was nothing to be embarrassed about, but she'd definitely choked out there tonight. This set the stage for an interesting Regional competition.

# CHAPTER 16

*Pro: An unexpected turn of events creates an opportunity for success.*
*Con: It's hard to be happy when your teammate is suffering.*

"So then he bought me red vines. How cute is he?" Maddie gushed to her friends at the rink. They were supposed to be warming up, but she couldn't stop talking about her movie date with Dylan the night before. Her mom had dropped them off at the theater and picked them up, but they'd been allowed to watch *When the Game Stands Tall* without anyone else around. Dylan reached for her hand as soon as the lights went down. Maddie still didn't get tired of reliving the memory.

"Adorbs," Alyssa said, passing Maddie's phone back to her. She'd snapped a selfie of herself and Dylan when the movie was over. Not the best shot ever, but it would have to do.

"What does Sydney think about all of this?" Taylor glanced over her shoulder, as if Sydney lurked nearby. But she wasn't even on the ice yet. Maddie hadn't seen her in the locker room, either.

"Ladies, enough talk. Let's get to work." Max clapped his hands and motioned for them to start skating.

Practice was intense. Maddie had little time to think about Dylan or Sydney or anything else, except keeping her skates moving. Max ran them through a series of drills to improve their agility and increase their cardiovascular strength. Maddie knew this would be their last week of tough workouts before they started to taper toward regionals. But that didn't help her now.

At the end of practice, the girls were cooling down and getting ready to stretch when the doors opened and Sydney came in, wearing her school clothes. Her face was red and her eyes puffy, like she'd been crying.

The girls exchanged worried glances when they heard "stress fracture" and "required to rest." While Mr. Gray insisted there must be some mistake and demanded a second opinion, Maddie stood up and spoke to Sydney.

"What's going on, Sydney?"

"I have a stress fracture in my leg. Overtraining, the doctor said." Sydney bit her lip and shoved her hands in the back pockets of her skinny jeans.

"I'm sorry," Maddie said. "That's a bummer."

Sydney shrugged. "It doesn't matter. I'll be back on the ice again soon."

Maddie didn't know what else to say. Wasn't she going to get some help for her other issues now that she couldn't skate?

Sydney walked away without another word. A few minutes later, she and her parents left the rink. The girls were silent for about two seconds before they burst out in a flurry of conversation.

Taylor was clearly overjoyed by this new development. While the rest pretended to be concerned, because they weren't supposed to be happy their teammate was injured, they knew this improved their chances of advancing in the competition. Taylor had struggled all season with her confidence and didn't conceal her excitement about what this could mean for her if there was one less competitor around.

Max and Elise interrupted their chatter with a few reminders to respect Sydney's privacy and not speculate about what might happen next. Their admonishment fell on deaf ears. This would be all the girls talked about until some other drama came their way. Maddie vowed silently to speak with Sydney about getting some help. When regionals were over, of course.

Besides, things were going so well with Dylan and she didn't want to mess it up. Dylan probably knew what was going on, but it wasn't his fault and he certainly couldn't fix it. He'd become the top scorer for the soccer team and they were on their way to playoffs. After the movie, he'd asked her to the homecoming dance. There was no way she was going to get involved with Sydney and her problems right now. Especially since Sydney made it pretty clear that she didn't want any help.

**\*\*\*\*\*\*\*\*\*\*\*\*\*\*\*\*\*\*\***

The homecoming dance was like a little slice of normal teenage life in the middle of an intense, highly competitive skating season. Delaney was the only freshman girl Maddie knew who was also going to the dance. Delaney came over and they got ready together. Delaney wore a short, bright red dress and Mom helped pin her hair up in a French twist. Maddie wore a sleeveless, royal blue dress and blew her hair out completely straight. They were finishing their makeup when the doorbell rang. Dylan and Michael, Delaney's date and Dylan's teammate, looked hot in their pastel dress shirts, gray pants, and bow ties.

"Rocking the bow ties, I love it," Delaney squealed from the bottom of the stairs.

"You look great," Dylan said with a smile.

"Thanks." Maddie instantly felt shy, especially when Dylan offered her a corsage for her wrist. Michael had one for Delaney, too, and the foursome posed for pictures in front of the Boones's fireplace. Maddie's parents had consented to letting Michael drive them to the dance, which was a huge deal. Zak would be there, too, but Maddie hoped she wouldn't see much of him. They didn't need a big brother chaperoning their first dance together.

The school auditorium was completely transformed. Maddie

couldn't believe it. But the streamers and balloons, even the spinning disco ball, were nothing compared to how she felt when Dylan pulled her into his arms for the first slow song of the night. His breath was warm against her cheek and she detected just a hint of spearmint, probably from a mint or a tic tac. She kept her hands on his shoulders and concentrated on not stepping on his toes.

"Relax," he said, leading her in a slow circle. "This is supposed to be fun."

Maddie looked up into his eyes. "I am having fun, just a little nervous."

"Me, too. I've never taken a girl to a dance before."

Maddie's heart soared. "For real?"

"For real." Dylan slid his hands around her waist and pulled her closer. Maddie thought her heart was going to beat right out of her chest.

After the last song, Michael and Delaney drove them to Maddie's house. Michael conveniently drove off, meaning Dylan would have to walk home. Maddie couldn't help wondering if they'd arranged that ahead of time. Her pulse sped up as he walked her toward the door. She hoped her dad wasn't waiting on the other side.

Dylan took both her hands in his, a smile playing at the corners of his mouth as he stared at her. "Thanks for going with me. I had a great time tonight, Maddie."

"Me, too," she whispered, trying so hard not to stare at his lips.

He dipped his head and she closed her eyes, sighing as his lips met hers. A shiver of delight ran through her as his lips lingered on hers, incredibly soft, just as she'd imagined. He pulled back and she opened her eyes.

"I should go. Good night." He squeezed her hands and walked back down the driveway.

"Good night," she whispered. Somehow she managed to find her voice. She stared after him until she couldn't see the back of his pink shirt in the darkness. *Wow*. She touched her fingers to her lips. She couldn't wait to tell the girls about this.

\*\*\*\*\*\*\*\*\*\*\*\*\*\*\*\*\*\*\*

On the ice the next day, tensions were high. If Maddie hoped to tell her friends all the details of the dance, Max put a stop to that very quickly. She got to the rink early, since she was excused from PE class and used that time on the rink, instead. But when she walked in and saw Max setting up the pole harness, she knew it was going to be a long afternoon.

They were fortunate that Max was certified to use the pole harness and Maddie knew she should be grateful. But it was the hardest workout of her life when he made her use that thing. Even though they'd dropped their early morning workouts, it was still all she could do to drag herself through school, try to stay healthy, and get her homework done.

Maddie dropped her stuff in the locker room and changed into her practice clothes. Maybe if she volunteered to go first, she could get the harness training over with and move on. Grabbing her skates, she hurried out to the rink.

"Maddie, I knew I could count on you to get out here first," Max said, unhooking the harness from the giant fishing pole he would hold while he skated alongside the girls.

"I hate that thing," Maddie grumbled, sitting down on the bench to lace up her skates.

"Now, now, this is for your own good," Max said.

Elise joined him on the ice so she could help the girls put the harness on and take it off. Maddie's palms felt clammy just looking at it. Even though she was skilled enough to not fall, jumping in the air on skates with someone holding you at the end of a pole still freaked her out.

The other girls were starting to come in to the arena as Maddie tugged her tights down over her skates and fastened the strap underneath the boots. Taking a few warm-up laps, she tried to mentally prepare herself for the workout ahead. *You can do this. They only want what's best for you.*

Skating over to Elise, Maddie drew a deep breath and let it out. "I'm ready."

"That's what we like to hear." Elise helped her wrap the harness around her shoulders, securing the strap around her waist. Then she hooked it to the pole and skated out of the way. "Okay, you guys are all set."

Max skated alongside her, keeping the tension on the harness low until they were able to increase their speed. It was a delicate balance, skating together and matching their strokes so he could eventually help propel her into the full rotations for her triple-triple combo.

"Okay, I'm ready," Maddie said, picking up speed. She glided backward then planted her toe pick and jumped into the air.

"Go, go, good, keep going," Max called out, using the harness to tug her body the way it needed to go. She felt awkward and jerky, as if they worked against each other. She touched down but couldn't go straight into the next jump. He guided her out of it so she wouldn't do a face plant on the ice.

"That was a nice first attempt," Max said. "Stop fighting me and let me do my part, okay?"

Maddie nodded, trapping her lower lip behind her front teeth. She didn't want to admit that she was terrified. But Max wasn't stupid. He could probably see it written all over her face.

After several more attempts, Maddie finally nailed the triple-triple combo with the help of Max and the harness.

"Woot! Woot!" Taylor cheered from across the ice. "That was epic, Maddie."

"Nice job, Maddie," Max said. "Let's end on a good jump and give you a chance to recover."

"Thank you," Maddie breathed a sigh of relief and skated toward the boards and her water bottle.

"That was great," Elise said, skating along with her. "Didn't it feel great?"

Maddie shrugged. "I guess. I still don't feel confident enough to land it in competition, though."

"But you've made so much progress. Just today, I saw a huge improvement in your speed and height. Don't worry, you'll get there."

"I'm not crazy about my double Axel, triple toe combo, either." Maddie skated to a stop and twisted the cap off her water bottle.

"Sometimes I think half the battle is silencing the voices in your head," Elise said.

Maddie dipped her chin, swirling the water around in her mouth. Elise was right about that.

"Sure, you're nervous about landing a huge combo in a major competition. You wouldn't be normal if that didn't scare you just a little. But we know you can nail it and we want you to know that, too."

"Most of the time, I see myself doing it right. But then competition rolls around and I—"

"You can do this, Mads. We believe in you." Elise skated off to help Taylor put the harness on, leaving Maddie alone with her thoughts. Especially now that Sydney probably couldn't skate, Maddie knew she had a shot at doing well at regionals. Alyssa would still skate, but there was a chance it would be her last competition if her family didn't figure out a way to finance her skating.

Taylor had really stepped up her focus and had an awesome free skate choreographed. There would be some strong competition both from within ECSC and from the skaters they competed against in Spokane. However, hosting regionals and skating on their home ice would give everybody a big advantage. Just the idea of performing in front of her friends and family on the same rink where she spent hours practicing sent a shot of adrenaline racing through her. This was an incredible opportunity, one she couldn't afford to mess up with her silly negative thinking.

# CHAPTER 17

*Pro: A great skater performs her best, lives in the moment and lets the pieces fall where they may.*
*Con: What if those pieces don't include a gold medal?*

The Emerald City Skate Club had rolled out the red carpet as hosts of the Pacific Northwest regional competition. The normally quiet, unassuming rink was crawling with dozens of skaters who were competing at every level. The crowd assembled for the short programs was enthusiastic and the seats were filled with parents, grandparents, and siblings. The tension and excitement were almost palpable.

Maddie had tried not to succumb to the superstitious rituals that a lot of skaters embraced, but she just couldn't help herself at this point. She tried to do everything exactly the same before a competition now. Her parents fixed the same dinner the night before, even though Zak grumbled that he never wanted to see chicken Parmesan again as long as he lived. She wanted to listen to Katy Perry as she was falling asleep, but decided changing her bedtime playlist the night before regionals was a little risky. She always mentally rehearsed all the elements of both routines, but this time she fell asleep before she even got to the free skate.

The day of competition, she put her warm ups on the same way and wore a silver pair of ice skates on a chain around her neck. She'd heard that Michele Kwan had a good luck charm that she never took off, either. Who could go wrong imitating the greatest skater who ever lived? The weather outside was unusually cold for October in the Northwest and Maddie worried about her asthma flaring up. She packed extra water and an extra rescue inhaler, just in case.

Later on, at the rink, Sydney stood at the edge of the ice right before Maddie warmed up.

"Good luck, Maddie." Sydney smiled and offered her a fist bump. "I'll be cheering for you."

Maddie smiled back, bumping her fist against Sydney's. "Thanks."

Sydney's doctor wouldn't allow her to compete or even practice, so she'd become a very devoted cheerleader. Maddie had never said another word about Sydney's eating issues, but she hoped this stress fracture was a wakeup call.

Although it would be easy to get caught up in how the other skaters performed, or even what they were doing during warm ups, Maddie knew better than to watch too closely. The top four advanced to Sectionals in California right before Thanksgiving. That was a given. It was her job to make sure she did everything she could to be one of those top four.

But the fierce competitor inside couldn't help but notice when other skaters did well. Alyssa skated first, surprising herself and everyone else, with the best short program she'd ever skated. The day before, she'd also received an anonymous scholarship, covering her expenses for this season and allowing her to continue skating indefinitely.

Maddie skated around the ice, taking her time, enjoying the sound of her edges against the ice. She knew she'd done everything she could to prepare for this competition. Her coaches, her parents and even Sydney had told her again and again that she needed to be in the moment and relax.

"Enjoy the artistic aspect of skating: clean lines, relaxed, fluid movements, the adrenaline rush of performing," Max called to her, hands cupped around his mouth to form a megaphone. It was like he could read her mind sometimes.

Blocking out everything else, Maddie skated to the center of the ice when the announcer called her name. She's skated on this ice for countless hours, without the applause and adoration of hundreds of pairs of eyes. It unnerved her a little to hear all the added noise in the same place she practiced, but somehow she'd have to find a way to use that to her advantage.

The music began and she danced across the ice, sashaying her way toward her opening jump combo. Once again, she abandoned the triple-triple in favor of a safer, more technically sound jump. A beautiful landing elicited an appreciative "oh" from the crowd and she knew she had made a great decision. A baby in the crowd screamed during her double Axel and she faltered, but with only a slight deduction. Her layback spin was phenomenal. She'd definitely earn extra marks there. With the more complicated jumps she'd landed in the last forty-five seconds, she'd definitely garner additional points for difficulty from judges.

Coming off the ice, she caught Dylan's eye and he flashed a thumbs up. Her already-pounding heart shifted into overdrive. No matter what the scores revealed, having him in the crowd was the best thing about the whole night. After everyone skated, Maddie hugged her family and both of her coaches. She trailed the first-place skater by only a couple of points.

\*\*\*\*\*\*\*\*\*\*\*\*\*\*\*\*\*\*\*\*

Day two of the regional competition, Maddie woke up and relished the fact that she'd slept in her own bed. Downstairs, Mom was fixing an awesome breakfast and not something from room service or a strange restaurant. Traveling to new places and skating on strange ice was all part of being an elite figure skater, and someday that might be her lifestyle, but today she'd get to skate on her home ice. Kicking off the covers, she stretched and yawned. It was going to be a great day.

Her family spent the morning trying to keep her as distracted as possible. She even helped Emily take care of a few of the pets in the neighborhood before it was time to eat lunch and leave for the rink.

By the time she warmed up, Maddie knew she had an excellent chance of advancing. A first place finish was so close, she could almost taste it. A win tonight meant she was one step closer to nationals, too.

Waiting for everyone else to skate felt like torture. Girls whom she thought would do well faltered, missing jumps and performing mediocre spins. But she had to stay focused, so she forced herself to stop watching. Instead, she moved to the hallway outside the locker room and listened to music while she paced back and forth. A few of her elements still made her nervous, so she chased away the doubt by rehearsing the jump combos at the end of the hallway. These were the only activities that helped her pass the time. Otherwise she was too preoccupied with the skaters on the rink and the scores on the jumbotron.

Once she re-tied her skates and double checked that her tights were secure, her heart began to pound and the butterflies took flight in her stomach once again. She wiped her sweaty palms on a towel and then made her way toward the rink.

When her name was announced and the crowd began to cheer, she took her place at the center of the ice as she'd done many times before. This was it. Her big moment. The high-energy rhythm of the music combined with the thrill of her flawless opening jump combo gave her the confidence she needed to skate a clean program. Every stroke of her skates was one stroke closer to a dream come true. Before the last note played and she thrust her arms toward the ceiling, she knew she'd done what seemed unattainable a few short months ago.

She skated toward the edge of the rink, a smile stretched wide across her face. Chest heaving, she hugged Elise first and then Max.

"We're so proud of you, Maddie!" Elise squeezed her shoulders, eyes shining bright.

"Well done, Maddie." Max pulled her in for a bear hug, his voice gruff.

Maddie slipped on her skate guards and made her way to the kiss and cry, stopping to high-five friends and fellow skaters who filled the front row of the arena, clapping and cheering.

Taking a seat, Maddie sipped her water and waited for what seemed like an eternity for the numbers to go up. Max's knee bounced up and down, knocking into hers. Elise squeezed her water bottle so tight that it crinkled in protest.

It was worth the wait. The judges' marks were incredible. First place. Maddie squealed and clapped her hands. She couldn't help but jump up and throw her arms around Elise first and then Max. She did it! She'd won the competition on her home ice, in front of her family, friends and Dylan. Next stop: sectionals with Alyssa, Taylor, and Emily at her side. Winning felt better than she'd imagined. Now she was in fact one step closer to making her dream come true.